"You're
of the (

The robber jerked—startled, no doubt, although Longarm could not see his facial expression beneath that hood—and brought the muzzle of his revolver around toward Longarm. Any self-respecting robber would have been aiming toward the coach to begin with, of course.

Then he made his second mistake. And by far his worst one. He cocked his piece—it rightly should have been ready to fire to start with—and tried to shoot Custis Long in the face.

Before the man could trigger his Smith & Wesson Schofield, Longarm put a bullet in his chest and another in his belly. The first slug knocked him back a step. The second doubled him over with a cry of pain.

"You didn't . . . you didn't have to . . ."

By that time Longarm was on the ground in a crouch, looking around for the others.

He saw no one . . .

DON'T MISS THESE
ALL-ACTION WESTERN SERIES
FROM THE BERKLEY PUBLISHING GROUP

THE GUNSMITH by J. R. Roberts
Clint Adams was a legend among lawmen, outlaws, and
ladies. They called him . . . the Gunsmith.

LONGARM by Tabor Evans
The popular long-running series about Deputy U.S. Marshal
Custis Long—his life, his loves, his fight for justice.

SLOCUM by Jake Logan
Today's longest-running action Western. John Slocum rides
a deadly trail of hot blood and cold steel.

BUSHWHACKERS by B. J. Lanagan
An action-packed series by the creators of Longarm! The
rousing adventures of the most brutal gang of cutthroats
ever assembled—Quantrill's Raiders.

DIAMONDBACK by Guy Brewer
Dex Yancey is Diamondback, a Southern gentleman turned
con man when his brother cheats him out of the family fortune. Ladies love him. Gamblers hate him. But nobody pulls
one over on Dex . . .

WILDGUN by Jack Hanson
The blazing adventures of mountain man Will Barlow—
from the creators of Longarm!

TEXAS TRACKER by Tom Calhoun
J.T. Law: the most relentless—and dangerous—manhunter
in all Texas. Where sheriffs and posses fail, he's the best
man to bring in the most vicious outlaws—for a price.

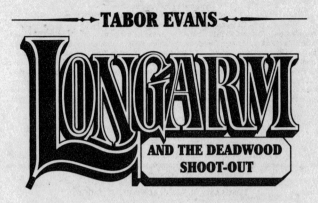

TABOR EVANS

LONGARM

AND THE DEADWOOD SHOOT-OUT

JOVE BOOKS, NEW YORK

THE BERKLEY PUBLISHING GROUP
Published by the Penguin Group
Penguin Group (USA) Inc.
375 Hudson Street, New York, New York 10014, USA

Penguin Group (Canada), 90 Eglinton Avenue East, Suite 700, Toronto, Ontario M4P 2Y3, Canada
(a division of Pearson Penguin Canada Inc.) • Penguin Books Ltd., 80 Strand, London WC2R 0RL,
England • Penguin Group Ireland, 25 St. Stephen's Green, Dublin 2, Ireland (a division of Penguin
Books Ltd.) • Penguin Group (Australia), 707 Collins Street, Melbourne, Victoria 3008, Australia
(a division of Pearson Australia Group Pty. Ltd.) • Penguin Books India Pvt. Ltd., 11 Community
Centre, Panchsheel Park, New Delhi—110 017, India • Penguin Group (NZ), 67 Apollo Drive,
Rosedale, Auckland 0632, New Zealand (a division of Pearson New Zealand Ltd.) • Penguin Books
(South Africa) (Pty.) Ltd., Rosebank Office Park, 181 Jan Smuts Avenue, Parktown North 2193,
South Africa • Penguin China, B7 Jiaming Center, 27 East Third Ring Road North,
Chaoyang District, Beijing 100020, China

Penguin Books Ltd., Registered Offices: 80 Strand, London WC2R 0RL, England

This is a work of fiction. Names, characters, places, and incidents either are the product of the author's
imagination or are used fictitiously, and any resemblance to actual persons, living or dead, business
establishments, events, or locales is entirely coincidental.

LONGARM AND THE DEADWOOD SHOOT-OUT

A Jove Book / published by arrangement with the author

PUBLISHING HISTORY
Jove edition / February 2013

Copyright © 2013 by Penguin Group (USA) Inc.
Cover illustration by Milo Sinovcic.

ISBN: 978-0-515-15305-7

JOVE®
Jove Books are published by The Berkley Publishing Group,
a division of Penguin Group (USA) Inc.,
375 Hudson Street, New York, New York 10014.
JOVE® is a registered trademark of Penguin Group (USA) Inc.
The "J" design is a trademark of Penguin Group (USA) Inc.

PRINTED IN THE UNITED STATES OF AMERICA

10 9 8 7 6 5 4 3 2 1

ALWAYS LEARNING   **PEARSON**

Chapter 1

Custis Long took the stone steps two at a time leading up to the Federal Building on Denver's Colfax Avenue, a tall man with broad shoulders and narrow hips. He was a study in brown, brown corduroy trousers, brown tweed coat, brown-and-white-checked shirt, and snuff-brown Stetson hat. He had a handlebar mustache, dark eyes flecked with gold, and a craggy face that women quite inexplicably found interesting. He wore a double-action Colt revolver in a black leather cross-draw rig.

He was feeling particularly good this morning. For more than a month he had been trying to convince a maddeningly lovely chorus girl at the Hansborough Theater that she should grant him the pleasure of her company, and finally she had wilted under the pressure of his repeated requests. This weekend after the Saturday night performances he would squire her out to dinner. And perhaps more. It was an understatement to say that he was looking forward to the engagement.

He entered the building and made his way down the corridor to a frosted-glass door marked U.S. MARSHAL.

The tall deputy entered the office suite, greeted Marshal William Vail's clerk with a cheery "Howdy, Henry," and hung his flat-crowned brown Stetson on the hat rack beside the door.

"Hello yourself, Longarm," Henry responded. Henry was a serious sort, slender and bespectacled. "Boss wants to see you," he said.

"I hope it's nothing serious," Longarm said, reaching up to smooth his hair and twist the ends of his mustache. "I got to get over to the barber shop this morning."

Henry shrugged as if to say he did now know what Billy Vail wanted. Longarm knew better. There was nothing that went on around this office that Henry was not privy to.

"Is anyone in with him?" Longarm asked.

Henry shook his head. "No, go on in."

Longarm paused outside Billy Vail's door and lightly tapped on it.

"Come in."

Longarm stepped inside. The marshal was seated behind his desk, poring over a stack of the paperwork that made most of his duties administrative ones while his deputies rode out to do the actual work of the office.

Billy Vail's appearance belied his abilities. He was round-faced, balding with a pink complexion and an innocent mien. He looked almost angelic but before coming to Denver had been a Texas Ranger and a salty one at that. Billy Vail could hold his own with a six-gun or a bad horse and many an outlaw had mistaken him for soft. That was an error they made only once.

Vail looked up from his papers and pushed them to one side. He motioned for Longarm to take a seat in one of the two chairs that faced the marshal's broad desk.

"I hope you don't have plans for the weekend," he said.

"I do, but that don't matter, Boss," Longarm said.

"Have you heard of the Salter gang?" Vail asked.

"Sure. Who hasn't. They're smart sons o' bitches. They rob in one territory an' escape into another where the law can't follow them, an' they never, ever make the mistake of doing anything that could put us onto them."

Billy smiled. "Well, they made their mistake this time. Or, rather, some very smart postal clerk got a step ahead of them."

Longarm's eyebrows went up in inquiry.

Billy's smile became even broader. "The gang has been taught that they take strongboxes and shake down passengers but they studiously avoid touching the U.S. mail pouches."

Longarm nodded. "That's the word about them, yeah."

"Well, this time a mail clerk in Cheyenne stuck a handful of mail into a strongbox that was being shipped to Deadwood. That shipment was basically minted coinage intended for the bank there. Payroll money for the most part. Salter or one of his people found out about it, something they have been particularly good at. The Salters hit that shipment and took the strongbox. Mind you, they did not intend to steal any undelivered mail, but thanks to that clerk in Cheyenne they did. There were six registered letters. The clerk, his name is Osgood, even wrote down the names and addresses of the senders and the addressees of those letters. So now thanks to him the Salters have stepped across the line and committed a crime under federal law."

"Osgood, you say?" Longarm said. "I'd like to shake that man's hand."

"You'll get the opportunity to do just that," Billy said. "I want you to go after the Salter gang and bring them in on charges of theft from the United States mails."

His date with Carrie Gibson was forgotten for the time being. This was much more interesting, especially since it went outside the routine of transporting prisoners to and from court dates.

"I can leave just as quick as the train schedule allows, Boss," he said.

"Good. See Henry for your vouchers. He has already been briefed." Which confirmed what Longarm already suspected about Henry's pretended ignorance of the assignment.

"Right away, Boss." Longarm stood and touched a finger to his forehead, then spun around and headed for the door.

Chapter 2

Cheyenne lay pretty much due north from Denver yet the fastest way to get there was to take a train east on the prairie to Julesburg, then another straight west on the UP tracks to Cheyenne. It was assumed that one of these days some enterprising railroader would build a line direct from Cheyenne to Denver. One of these days. Longarm had that same faint hope every time he had to go to Cheyenne—which was one of his favorite towns; it was only getting there that was a pain in the ass.

On his way to one of his favorite towns he wiled away the time with one of his favorite hobbies, that being the admiration of beautiful women.

As it happened there were three seated in his car. Well, two and a half. One of them lost points because of her thick ankles.

The most delightful of the females available to be admired was a half-grown filly whose age he guessed would be something in the neighborhood of twelve or thirteen. She was young and pretty and flighty, flitting from seat to window to platform and back again, eagerly chatting with her mother and then dashing off again on another adventure.

There was not a lewd thought in Longarm's mind when he watched her. Just the sheer joy of admiring youthfully vivacious beauty. Had he ever been that young and carefree, he wondered. Surely not. Never mind that. The child was a pleasure to admire.

And her mother was not bad herself. Mama had soft brown hair tucked into a close-fitting bonnet. Both she and the little girl wore nicely tailored dusters so he could not judge Mama's figure but no matter. She was pretty enough that her body seemed almost unimportant. Longarm grinned at the thought. Almost!

It was well past dark when the coach rattled into Julesburg, glowing coke cinders dropping out of the night sky onto the sleepy-eyed passengers, most of whom would be changing to other trains here as Julesburg was the terminus for the Denver branch.

"This way to the Union Pacific mainline," a uniformed conductor bawled. "This way to the omnibuses. Eastbound passengers that way"—he pointed—"westbound, follow me."

The woman with the thick ankles turned toward the eastbound platform. The mother and little girl trudged sleepily toward the horse-drawn omnibus that would take them to the platform for westbound trains.

Inside the close confinement of the omnibus Longarm could not avoid overhearing them when the child tugged on her mother's sleeve and in a rather loud whisper asked if she could have something to eat.

"When we get to Grandma's, sweetie," the mother told her.

"But, Mama, I'm hungry now."

The woman's expression hardened and she looked furtively around to see if anyone else in the coach was paying attention to this exchange.

"Not now," she hissed through clenched teeth.

"Ma . . ."

"We don't have money for such so be quiet, Liberty."

The little girl wilted on the rough cloth of the omnibus seat. "Yes, Mama."

It was but a short ride to the westbound platforms. The coach emptied out there. Most of the passengers filed into the waiting room. A few, including mother and child, waited outside on the platform even though at this middle-of-the-night hour it was fairly chilly out there in the night air.

Longarm went inside the terminal and spotted a butcher boy hawking dried-out sandwiches and somewhat fresher crullers. He bought three of the crullers and carried them out onto the platform.

"Ma'am," he said, bowing. "I made a mistake in there. I gave the boy too much money an' he didn't have change so I took three t' make it all come out even, never mind that I only want the one of 'em. Would you think me too forward if I was t' offer these extras t' you an' the child there?"

"Thank you, sir, but I couldn't."

"I understand that, ma'am, but they're way more than I can handle. Reckon I'll just have t' throw them away if you won't take them." He feigned a sigh. "I surely do hate t' waste perfectly good food."

Like most women of his experience, this lady, too, abhorred waste. "If you are sure . . ."

He smiled. "Downright positive, ma'am."

"In that case . . . just so they do not go to waste . . ."

He handed over the spare crullers, touched the brim of his Stetson, and wandered off to the other end of the platform to eat his sticky, somewhat-too-sweet cruller by himself.

Chapter 3

Longarm yawned and stretched, then picked up his carpetbag and looked around for a hack. Cheyenne in the middle of the day was busy, wagons and heavy drays hauling goods to and from the railroad. He stood on the platform and considered where to go next. The first thing he needed to do would be to learn more about the robbery that led to the Salter outfit taking as yet undelivered U.S. mail. He needed to speak with the local law and to the mail clerk. Probably he would need to go to Deadwood.

First things first, though. He needed some lunch after the long haul east from Denver and back west again. After lunch he should talk with the county sheriff, then the mail clerk, then . . . he would see how things developed. He would . . .

"Mister." He felt a tug on his sleeve. "Mister?"

He looked down into the wide blue eyes and freckles of the little girl from the trains. He smiled; he could not help it. "Yes, miss?"

"My gramma wants to see you."

Longarm raised an eyebrow.

"Over there," the child said, pointing to a handsome and obviously very expensive phaeton complete with driver and coachman, both wearing matching white shirts and bright yellow vests.

"That is your grandmother's rig?"

The kid nodded and took Longarm by the hand.

"One second, please." He stepped over to the station agent's cubicle and set his carpetbag inside with a quick, "Watch this, will you?" Then he went with the little girl.

Gramma turned out to be a woman in her fifties or thereabouts. Tall, slender, with silver-gray hair, high cheekbones, and striking green eyes, an ice queen with the look of someone who had been pampered and rich all her life. She was a beauty despite her age and she obviously knew it. She held herself rigidly upright.

The little girl's mother was already seated in the phaeton. The coachman was busy loading luggage into the boot.

"You are the gentleman who was so kind to my daughter and granddaughter, I believe," the older lady said. "I want you to know that we . . . that they . . . are not beggars. They were robbed while they were in Denver. Robbed of everything. The only thing the scoundrel missed, or did not want, was their return train tickets. That is why they were in such desperate circumstances when you found them and took pity on them."

"Why, ma'am, if I'd've known that I would've set them both up to a good feed," Longarm said. "I'm sorry they didn't mention it."

"I believe you would have done exactly that," the lady said. "Permit me to introduce myself, sir. I am Cornelia Blaise. This is my daughter, Melody Carmichael, and my granddaughter, Liberty."

Longarm doffed his Stetson and made a leg toward Mrs. Blaise. When he straightened up he said, "I'm Deputy U.S. Marshal Custis Long, ma'am, an' I'm pleased t' make your acquaintance."

"A marshal! My goodness. And quite the gallant, too. It is approaching the noon hour, Marshal Long. Would you be free to join us for luncheon?"

"I'd be pleased t' do that, Miz Blaise. If I wouldn't be intruding on your family time."

"It would be our pleasure, Marshal, and the least we could do to repay your kindness."

"That ain't necessary, ma'am," he said.

"Please, mister," Liberty pleaded, tugging at his coat sleeve. "Please come. I never met a real marshal before. Please?"

Longarm looked down into the little girl's eyes. That was enough to make up his mind. He smiled. "Can I sit next t' you if I come?"

The child hopped up and down with pleasure. "You can. I promise."

"Well, in that case . . ."

Chapter 4

Longarm stared. He could not help himself. The Blaise
mansion was larger than some—hell, it was larger than
most—hotels he had stayed in. It sat on three acres or so
of carefully groomed lawn on the edge of Cheyenne, out
past the territorial capitol building. It was three stories tall
with a small porch and white columns at the front. A doorman waited for them as the phaeton rolled through the
wrought-iron gate and up a curving, graveled driveway.

"Welcome to Blaise House," the grand dame said.

"Yes, welcome," Mrs. Carmichael echoed. Liberty
just grinned and hugged Longarm's arm.

The phaeton crunched to a halt on the gravel and the
coachman jumped down from his perch to open the door
and assist the ladies to the ground. Liberty made a game
of hopping down. And Longarm was left to get down
without professional assistance while the doorman dashed
out to fetch in the luggage.

Inside, the entry was a hall large enough to hold dances.
The furnishings were dark and heavy. The lighting was

from electrified chandeliers, suggesting that Blaise House had its own generating plant because Longarm was fairly sure the town had none. Even Denver had few such plants. A setup like that would surely cost a fortune. But then the Blaise family quite obviously had a fortune to cover it.

"We will be in the parlor, Donald. Please inform us when dinner is ready."

"Yes, ma'am." The doorman, who apparently performed double duty as the butler, too, actually bowed his way out.

Longarm wondered if he should run into town and buy a formal outfit so he would be properly attired here.

"This way please, Mr. Long," the grand lady said, taking his arm and guiding him through the foyer to an equally large and impressive parlor. It was furnished with large, overstuffed pieces. The far wall was open to a glassed sunroom with a concert piano in the center.

She led him to a sofa, Liberty clinging to his other arm, and settled him there with Liberty tucked in close beside him.

"Coffee, Mr. Long?"

"That would be nice, ma'am, thank you." Actually a shot or two of rye whiskey would have been better after a night spent on the rails, but coffee would do for the moment.

Mrs. Blaise nodded in the direction of the doorway and the butler instantly stepped into the room. "Coffee, Donald."

"Yes, ma'am."

It was only a matter of seconds before Donald came in wheeling a cart with silver service and china cups. The coffee was steaming hot, the cream thick and heavy. It occurred to Longarm that a fellow could get used to living like this . . . from the master's point of view, that is, less so from that of the servants.

The coffee was predictably excellent, the dinner that followed equally fine, the meal rich and heavy. As they were nearing the conclusion of the feast—a feast for most folks but normal enough here, he guessed—Liberty left her chair at Longarm's side and ran to the head of the table. She leaned close and whispered in her grandmother's ear. Mrs. Blaise gestured to Donald and in turn whispered in his ear. Then she smiled and patted Liberty's cheek. Liberty jumped up and down with joy and ran back to Longarm.

"You can stay here with us, Mr. Marshal. Isn't that fine?"

"But I . . ."

"It is all arranged, Mr. Long," Mrs. Blaise said before he could finish. "My coachman has already been dispatched to bring your bag from the depot, and Donald is having a bedroom prepared for you." She smiled. "Believe me, we have enough guest rooms that you will be no intrusion."

"Please, Mr. Marshal? Please?" Liberty clung to his arm and practically swooned with excitement.

He looked down into those guileless blue eyes and melted. "All right," he said. "But I can only stay the one night. I have work to do, you know."

The little girl kissed the back of his hand and shivered with delight while her mother pretty much ignored the whole thing.

Chapter 5

Marcus Carmichael, Liberty's father, put in an appearance about six o'clock, arriving in a light runabout drawn by a sleek, black trotter. Carmichael himself was plump and sleek, with oiled hair and a diamond stickpin. He accepted Longarm's presence in his house as a commonplace occurrence. Both his welcome and his handshake were perfunctory, and he immediately retired to his study with the instruction that he be called when supper was served.

Longarm visited with the ladies and spent most of his afternoon and evening playing card games with Liberty.

Supper was light but the service was formal. Afterward Longarm retired upstairs where a room had been prepared for him. There had been no invitation for him to join Carmichael in the study for brandy and cigars. It was a lack Longarm could live with. His only purpose for staying was to please Liberty. The child was such a joy that he almost wished for a daughter of his own.

But then, he realized with a chuckle, it was more convenient to borrow one.

Before she was up to bed Liberty went onto her tiptoes
and gave Longarm a good-night kiss.

The child just plain melted his heart; that was the truth
of the matter.

Upstairs, tucked away at the back of the third floor,
the family being somewhere below, he sat in the bedroom
rocking chair long enough for a smoke and a nip of rye
from the bottle he carried in his carpetbag, then he stripped,
blew out the lamp, and crawled between the fresh, sunlight-
scented sheets.

He was asleep almost immediately.

He came awake again to a light knocking on his door. In
this genteel upper-class house there was no need for him
to reach for the .45 he had placed on the bedside table.
He sat up and reached for it anyway and had the revolver
in hand when he stood and padded to the doorway.

Lamplight shone beneath the door.

"Who is it?" he asked, standing to the side of the door.

"Cornelia," the answer came back.

Longarm's eyebrows went up. "Yes, I, uh, just a
moment." He hurriedly put the revolver back into its
leather, then returned to the door and pulled it open.

Cornelia Blaise, sometimes known as Gramma, stood
there holding a hurricane lamp. She was wearing a sleep-
ing gown of pale silk with pearls and fancywork sewn on.
The gown came to her throat and had long sleeves, but
the way the silk clung to her curves—and Cornelia Blaise
had what Custis Long considered to be quite splendid
curves—it managed to be sexy as hell.

"May I come in?"

Longarm stepped back and the lady swept into his
bedroom.

She very carefully set the lamp onto the bedside table,

quite matter-of-factly shifting his Colt to one side when she did so.

When she turned to him the lamplight was behind her. He could see the outline of her figure through the back-lighted silk. Her legs were long and slim. Her breasts small and shapely, riding high on her chest despite her years.

Her hair was down, flowing loose and long. It caught the gleam of the lamplight and seemed almost to shimmer.

Longarm's cock had no notion of a houseguest's polite behavior. It immediately jumped to attention.

Cornelia looked down and saw the sudden bulge in his balbriggans.

The grand lady smiled and said, "Good. Would you like to fuck?"

Chapter 6

Longarm was too surprised to speak, but his pecker, lightly throbbing behind the thin cloth of his balbriggans, spoke for him.

Cornelia stepped forward. One arm crept around Longarm's neck. Her other hand very matter-of-factly gripped his cock. She lifted her face to his and kissed him, her tongue sliding into his mouth when she did so.

"Beautiful," she whispered.

Longarm lifted an eyebrow and the grand lady smiled and said, "Not you, dear. This is what I was thinking of." She squeezed his prick and laughed.

"Beautiful? Why, you ain't even seen it yet," Longarm said.

"We can correct that, can't we?" she asked.

"Uh-huh. Reckon we can at that."

Without waiting for more of an invitation, Cornelia unfastened the buttons at the neck of the balbriggans and slipped the undergarment off his shoulders. She pushed them down past his hips and let them drop to the floor around his ankles.

"Lovely," she said, looking down at the powerful erection that was standing tall down there. "See? I was right all along." She took hold of him and squeezed again.

"Careful what you're doin' there or you'll get a fistful of jism," he warned.

"I can think of better places for it," Cornelia said.

He reached up to the neck of her nightdress and felt for the closure. Found it at the back, hidden beneath her hair. He slipped the button free and the silky garment slithered to the floor under its own weight, pooling there in a cream-colored pile.

"Damn, woman, you're mighty fine," he observed. And indeed she was. Tall and slim and with only a hint of belly. Her tits were pale, the nipples small and pink. The bush at her crotch was a vee of gray fur, tightly curled and already moist with her juices.

Cornelia came to him, this time wrapping both arms around his neck. She raised herself on tiptoes and lifted one leg high. Longarm was surprised to find that she had easily impaled herself on his cock, taking him deep into her cunt while they stood belly to belly and lip to lip.

She kissed him, pulling his tongue into her hot mouth while she ground her hips against his.

Cornelia was able to take every inch of him, something that not every woman could handle. She rocked back and forth against him, his prick sliding in and out with the woman's motion.

Without warning she tightened her arms around his neck and lifted herself, wrapping her legs around Longarm's waist and driving herself onto him. He was holding her completely off the floor, his arms around her torso, her tits warm and soft on his chest.

He felt the heat of her pussy. Felt the slippery moisture

of her juices. Felt his own sap quickly rise in response to her.

Cornelia bit his ear but Longarm scarcely felt it. His concentration was on the exquisite sensations of being deep inside this handsome woman's body.

He groaned and shuddered as his come exploded into her. Cornelia began to shudder and moan as he did so. If she was faking her orgasm, he realized, she was doing one hell of a fine job of it.

He clung tightly to her, all of her weight on his sturdy frame as both of them came.

After another minute or so he sighed. Cornelia unwrapped herself from around him and dropped her feet to the floor once more. But she continued her hold around his neck, her mouth on his, her breath rapid and hot.

"Damn," she whispered when she pulled her face an inch or so away from his.

"Yeah," Longarm agreed.

"You are good, dearest," she said.

"Glad y' think so, ma'am."

The lady giggled and asked, "Do you think we can do it again?"

"You bet, but let's lie down an' try it this time."

She took his hand and led him onto the bed, placing herself wide open for his entry when he joined her.

Chapter 7

Cornelia stayed with him until dawn, then she slipped out of his room. When Longarm went downstairs for breakfast an hour later the woman acted like she scarcely knew him.

Liberty begged him to stay "just one more day," which Cornelia, with a twinkle in her eye, seconded, but he kissed the little girl on the forehead and declined the invitation.

"It's work that brought me up here, an' I'd best get to it."

"Finish your breakfast then and we shall drive you back into town," Cornelia said.

The distance was not so much that he could not walk it but he was glad enough for the offer. Donald fetched his bag downstairs and escorted him outside where a light wagon was waiting for him. Half an hour later he was deposited in front of the Cheyenne post office.

"Mornin'," he greeted the clerk on duty. Longarm showed his badge, then said, "I'm looking for a gent name of Osgood. I don't know his first name."

"That would be Clarence," the clerk said. "He's in the back sorting mail. Is this important?"

"Very," Longarm said.

The clerk frowned but said, "All right then. Come inside the cage. I'll take you to him."

Clarence Osgood turned out to be a burly, rather tough-looking man with hairy arms and heavy beard stubble. When Longarm introduced himself Osgood nodded and said, "I thought one of you fellows would be along. That's why I put that mail in the strongbox."

"That was good thinking," Longarm said.

Osgood grunted. "Look, Marshal, I been on the far side of the law a time or two before I found the Lord. Now I try to do right."

"Well, you did right this time," Longarm said. "My boss tells me you have information on the folks those letters were going to. I'd like that list if you don't mind."

"Why is that?" Osgood asked.

"That will be part of the evidence against these people when I bring them to trial," Longarm explained. "Dependin' on how things go, I might want t' get statements from them for the prosecutor t' use when it comes down to that."

Osgood grunted. "Yeah, that makes sense. Just a minute. I got the list in my locker. Wait here." He disappeared into the back of the post office and returned a minute later with an envelope that he handed to Longarm. "Is there anything else I can help with?" he asked.

Longarm shook his head and said, "Not that I can think of. But if I do, I'll be back."

"Anything," the postal worker said. "Anytime."

"Thanks." Longarm shook the man's hand and left. He retrieved his carpetbag from the lobby, where he had left it, and walked to the Laramie County sheriff's office.

"I'm hoping to find some information on the Salter gang," he told the tall, sun-bronzed sheriff. "Whatever you know, anything you know, would be a help because I don't know much of anything about them other than the fact that they are damned good at robbery."

Sheriff Bertram Rutter took Longarm into his office and motioned for him to have a seat. He went around behind his desk and settled into his swivel chair. He leaned back and asked, "Do you mind if I smoke while we talk?"

Longarm grinned. "Not if you don't mind if I do."

Rutter loaded a pipe and fired it up while Longarm nipped the twist off one of his cheroots. Rutter held a match for him to light the cigar and both men leaned back in their chairs.

"What little I know about the Salters," Rutter said, "comes from an article in a back-East newspaper. From Philadelphia. It was written by an Englishwoman who claimed she was able to interview the gang on the promise that she would not reveal their names or where they lived. They told her . . . allegedly, that is . . . told her that they rob in Wyoming and Nebraska but live in a different jurisdiction where they have committed no crimes and are not wanted."

"That would make it Dakota or Montana," Longarm observed.

"Right," Rutter said. "If they were telling the truth."

"And if the reporter really did get an interview like that. She could have made it all up."

"She could have," the sheriff agreed, "but hers is the only information we have."

"Is the reporter available for me to talk with?"

Rutter shrugged. "Who knows. I've never met her and

don't know if she is still out here. For all I know she could be back East again by now. Or all the way home to England. The article came out weeks ago."

"Do you have a copy?" Longarm asked.

"No, I don't, but maybe one of my people or someone over in the courthouse has one. I can ask around for you."

"I'd appreciate that," Longarm said.

"Other than that," Rutter said, "we know practically nothing about these people. The way they work, they seem to know what stages to hit. They never bother to steal an empty strongbox, only worthwhile targets. One or two of them will step out in front of the stage with shotguns leveled. They never speak. Not a word. They just motion with those shotguns. After the box has been thrown down they get the passengers out and rob them . . . still without saying a word out loud, mind you . . . then step aside and let the stage go on its way. They've never harmed anyone. They have gotten away with half a dozen of these robberies now."

"What do they look like?" Longarm asked. "After that many robberies you should have a pretty good description of them."

"Ha," Rutter grunted. "You would think so, wouldn't you? In fact we have no idea what they look like. They always wear full-length dusters buttoned to the throat plus flour-sack hoods covering their heads. They even wear gloves, more like gauntlets, to cover their hands and forearms. No one except this newspaper reporter has ever gotten a look at them."

"Assuming she really did," Longarm said.

"Exactly."

"Well, someone, somewhere, has to know some-damn-thing," Longarm said.

"I wish you luck finding them," Rutter said. "The robberies occurred outside my jurisdiction, but if there is any way I can help, Long, I'll be glad to do so."

"I thank you, Sheriff. What I'd like from you, if I may, would be the name of this Philadelphia newspaperwoman. Just in case she's still out this way."

"Of course," Rutter said. "Anything I can do. Anything at all."

Chapter 8

Longarm returned to the Cheyenne post office, but this time instead of Osgood he asked the clerk if he might see the Cheyenne postmaster.

"Look, mister, we got work to do here," the clerk complained.

"Yes," Longarm said agreeably, "and so do I. Mine includes talkin' with your postmaster. So you can politely point the way for me or I can discuss with your p'lice chief about charging you with obstruction of a federal officer in the performance o' his duties. I dunno. Maybe the judge will let you off with, say, ten or twenty days. Prob'ly no more'n a month." Longarm put on an innocent and open expression and smiled at the man.

The mail clerk blanched and stepped back away from his cage. "I, um . . . this way, please."

Longarm went inside the caged area and meekly followed the postal clerk to a tiny cubbyhole of an office that was protected by a door stout enough to stop at full-on assault by Viking warriors.

The postmaster was inside, caught reading the morning newspaper with his feet propped up on his desk. He did not bother dropping them to the floor until he saw that the clerk had brought a stranger with him. The man's shoes, Longarm noticed, were high-topped and shined to a gleam. Old-fashioned, he thought, and something of a fuddy-duddy.

"Who are you," the man challenged, "and what do you want?"

The clerk extracted himself from the situation and got the hell out of there. Longarm smiled again and fleetingly wished he could follow the clerk back to wherever the man went. Instead all he did was to introduce himself and show his badge.

"Sit. Go on. Sit down." The postmaster, T. Jonathon Jessup, vaguely motioned in the direction of an empty chair that sat in front of the desk.

Longarm sat.

"You would be here about the mail theft," the postmaster said, sounding quite certain about it.

Longarm nodded. "I am."

"Osgood will have told you everything we know," Jessup declared.

Longarm nodded again. "Almost everything, perhaps. But I have some questions for you, too."

"Fine, but be quick about it. I'm busy."

"So I see," Longarm drawled, making it clear that indeed he had seen the newspaper and the feet on the desk.

"Go on then. You have questions. Ask them."

"It isn't about this robbery so much as about your procedures. How would any of your people know what might be in the mail?"

"We wouldn't," Jessup said. "Not unless a package is insured. Then we might ask about the contents. Otherwise, nothing."

"So none of your people could know what is on those stagecoaches?" Longarm asked.

"No. They couldn't. Not at all."

Longarm grunted. Thought for a moment. "Who would?"

"Talk to the people who operate the coaches," Jessup suggested.

"And they would be . . . ?"

"Tom Delancey in the Fremont Stage Company office. It's across the street and down a block. There is a sign. Can't miss it."

"All right, I'll try him. But I did want to know about your procedures."

"Why?" Jessup wanted to know.

Longarm shrugged. "In something like this, Mr. Jessup, you cast your lines on the waters an' hope something rises to snap at one."

"Is that all then?"

"One more thing. Is Osgood the man who normally prepares the mail for shipment?"

Jessup nodded firmly. "He is."

"Good," Longarm said with a smile. "That probably means that none of your people are involved in this thing."

Jessup looked puzzled.

"Somebody knew to tip the gang off to what shipments they should hit," Longarm explained.

"Ah. Yes, of course." Jessup picked up his newspaper again. "Is that all then?"

"Yes. At least for the moment," Longarm said. "If there's anything else, I'll be back."

Jessup only grunted. It was obvious he did not particularly like the idea of any federal officer peeking behind the doors at his post office. It was equally obvious that he knew there was nothing he could do about it. "Have a good day." The man was already lost in his newspaper, feet up on the desk, before Longarm cleared the doorway.

Chapter 9

Thomas Arthur Delancey was young, strong, and harried. Longarm got the impression he was a man whose hard work and intelligence would serve him well in the future.

Longarm guessed Delancey was still in his twenties, perhaps even his early twenties, but he obviously knew his business and did it well. When Longarm introduced himself Delancey immediately set aside the clipboard loaded with shipping forms that he had been comparing against the pile of packages due to go out on the next Fremont Stage Company coach.

Delancey stuck his hand out to shake and said, "It's a pleasure to meet you, Long. Thanks for looking into this for us."

"You understand what the situation is, I assume," Longarm said.

Delancey nodded. "Of course. Until this recent robbery the only legal jurisdiction involved was local. Until there was mail included . . . Osgood told me what he had done . . . you had no authority to act. Now you do. Smart man, Osgood. I wish he would come to work for me here at Fremont. We could use more people with heads on their shoulders." He smiled. "I think some of my fellows keep theirs strictly inside their britches."

"I know the type," Longarm said.

"You'll be wanting to know how anyone could know there was cash on those coaches," Delancey said. "That would be the logical question."

"So it is," Longarm said.

"I wish I could tell you. But then if I knew, Marshal, there wouldn't be any more of these robberies, damn them."

"Fremont is on the hook for the losses?" Longarm asked.

"No, we have insurance. On the other hand, our insurance rates are bound to go up because of this. Fremont is not a large company, Marshal. We operate on a small margin. I suppose most transportation companies do, but a large outfit like Overland or Wells Fargo makes up in volume for what it lacks in profit margin. We don't have that luxury. We have only fourteen coaches covering six routes. We are solvent, but we can't afford to give anything away. These losses are hurting us."

"Do you think that could be deliberate on the part of the robbers? That is to say, do you think the purpose of the robberies is to damage Fremont Stage Company?"

"I have no reason to think so," Delancey said. "I don't know of anyone who would have cause to target us in particular. Besides, we're not the only company that has been hit by these people. Some of Hal Tyler's coaches have been robbed, too."

"Tyler?" Longarm said. "That's the first time I've heard that name. Who is he?"

"Hal is superintendent of the Bastrop line in Miles City. Good man, too. I know at least two of Hal's coaches have been hit. I never heard the details or what they might have been carrying on board, but I do know they were hit."

"Miles City," Longarm said. "That means Montana. And another jurisdiction where they robbed. I'll have t' talk to the man, I think, never mind that those robberies wouldn't be federal crimes. Sounds like the same gang involved though."

"Like I said, Hal is a good man. I'm sure he will help you if he can."

"Do you know where those coaches were bound?"

Delancey shook his head. "I don't. Sorry."

"Your losses, though," Longarm said. "Were they all on the same runs?"

"Yes, they were. They were all dispatched to Lead and Deadwood, all carrying coinage the banks there need to meet payrolls."

"Coins, not currency?"

Delancey nodded. "I suppose you know that almost everyone out here insists he be paid in coin. Those boxes would have held a little gold and a good amount of silver coins." His expression was tight when he added, "Most salaries are very small, you see. They would pay mostly in silver."

Longarm pulled at his chin and thought for a moment. "Heavy," he said.

"The silver, you mean. Yes, the boxes would have been very heavy, but in each case that I know of they were broken open on the spot after the coaches rolled on and the coins taken out. The coins could have been trans-ferred to saddlebags. The gang wouldn't necessarily have needed a wagon to transport the money, although a wagon would have been useful."

"What about the way the robbery was conducted? An' do you mind if I smoke?"

"Go ahead. My drivers tell me each time the robbers just suddenly appeared in front of them. They chose places on the road where there was a bend or a dip or something so the coach would just suddenly come upon this person standing there pointing a sawed-off shotgun at them. There would be one or two more standing beside the road, also with shotguns.

"None of them would say a word. Just gesture with the muzzles of those scatterguns. There are not too many drivers or guards who would make a play once that happened. And don't forget, our people, like pretty much everyone in the business, has the protection of the passengers as our first priority. They did right to drop the box and drive on."

"Your insurance company," Longarm said, "would they have knowledge of the contents of those boxes? Ahead of time, I mean."

"No, we have blanket coverage for our losses regardless of what we are carrying."

"But your people would have to know what was in the boxes," Longarm said.

"Yes, of course, but never ahead of time. The bank would bring their shipment to us at the last minute."

"And their insurance?" Longarm asked.

"I wouldn't know about that," Delancey said.

"What did the robbers look like?" Longarm asked, changing the subject. He pulled out a cheroot and lighted it.

"We have no descriptions, not even of voices since they

did not speak. They wore long dusters buttoned to the
throat. Sacks over their heads. Long gloves. Boots showing at ground level. Never anything that would identify
them, at least nothing that any of my people saw."

"Was anything found at the scenes afterward? Dis-
carded masks or anything like that?"

"No, just the empty strongboxes. They took everything else with them."

"What about horse tracks?" Longarm asked.

"Oh, it was easy enough to see where their horses had
been tied. Droppings and all that sort of thing, but no
indication of how many horses there had been or if some
were pack animals while some were saddle horses."

Longarm frowned in thought while he puffed on his
cheroot for a moment. "Always the same bank doing the
shipping?"

Delancey smiled. "I thought of that, too. A bank
employee might have tipped them off. But no, the ship-
pers were two different Cheyenne banks and one from
Denver. And since the shipments were all consigned at
the last minute . . . I suppose to keep information from
getting out ahead of time . . . there would not have been
time enough for any of my people to notify robbers a
hundred miles or more away."

"Obviously you've given this a great deal of thought,"
Longarm said.

"Of course. The bastards are hurting Fremont. That
means they are hurting me, and I just plain resent it,"
Delancey said.

"Can't say as I blame you," Longarm told him, taking
another drag on his cigar. "If I think of any more questions, I'll be back."

"Anytime, Marshal. I'll be happy to do anything I can

to find these sons of bitches and put them behind bars where they belong."

"Thanks." Longarm offered his hand again and left the Fremont Stage Company office. The day was wearing on and he was getting hungry. He figured he could chew on what he knew while he chewed on some beef.

Chapter 10

"Slab o' beef and a mess o' taters," Longarm said. "Fry the both of them in tallow. Make 'em nice an' crispy-like."

"You want some pie while you're waiting for your meal?" the waitress offered. It reminded Longarm that this was a railroad town, taking dessert first being a habit of the train crews.

"No, thanks," he said. "Just coffee."

The woman nodded and set a cup on the counter. She quickly filled it, then headed for the kitchen to turn in his order.

When his food came the steak was tough but tasty, the yellow fat suggesting it was grass-fed beef and probably local, the mountain of potatoes just the way he liked them. Longarm ate, then slid off the café stool and dropped a half dollar beside his plate. He nodded to the very busy waitress and ambled outside, pausing in the doorway to nip the twist off one of his cheroots. He struck a lucifer and lighted the slim cigar, then headed for one of the two Cheyenne banks that had lost shipments.

"You will want to speak with our comptroller, Mr. Walters," one of the counter clerks said when Longarm introduced himself. "This way, please."

The clerk led him to a small office tucked away at the back of the bank.

George Walters was probably in his early thirties, already balding. He was slightly pudgy. The hand he offered Longarm to shake was small and as soft as a woman's, but his attitude was brisk and businesslike. Longarm got the impression that Walters knew his business.

"And, ah, what is it I can do for you today, Marshal?" Walters asked, motioning Longarm to a chair.

"The robberies," Longarm said. "I need t' know who in the bank knew about those shipments. When they were going an' what was in them."

Walters pursed his lips and steepled his hands under one of his several chins.

Longarm did not know whether he was pondering if he should answer the question or searching his memory for the answer.

"I knew," Walters said after deliberation. "Our chief teller knew. The president knew." He was silent for another moment or two, then added, "I believe that would be everyone."

"Who took the coins to the Fremont office?"

"Again, Marshal, I did."

"You carried all that coin?" Longarm asked. "You yourself?"

"Oh, I see what you mean. No, we have a handyman who works here. Davey something. Fitzsimmon, I think. Donnalson—that would be our head teller—Donnalson and I prepared the shipment. Counted the coins and sorted them. Packed them in canvas bags. They weighed between thirty-five and forty pounds per shipment.

I escorted them to the Fremont office. Davey did the actual carrying using a hand truck."

"So there were four of you who were aware of the shipments before they left Cheyenne."

Walters nodded.

"Were they all bound for the same recipient?" Longarm asked.

"No. One was shipped to the Golden Star in Lead, Dakota Terrtory. Oddly enough, sir, the Golden Star produces silver. The others all went to the Stella Mining Company in Deadwood." He frowned and shook his head. "That lone shipment consigned to the Golden Star was an especially heavy loss as the same box held coins intended for Stella."

"Did all the shipments include specie for the Stella payroll?"

"Yes, they did," Walters said.

"So someone at the Stella company would know the money was on its way?"

"Yes, of course. They ordered the shipments, after all."

"How did they place the orders?" Longarm asked.

"By telegraph, of course."

"So a telegraph operator would know, too."

"No, not at all. The wires are coded, telling us when they want a shipment and how much. The telegraphers at either end would not know what those messages contained."

Longarm nodded and reached for a cheroot.

"Please don't smoke in here," Walters said.

"Sorry. What about your insurance?" Longarm asked. "Would your local agent know about the shipments?"

"Not in advance," Walters said. "Naturally they had to know after the fact, but we took out no additional coverage for these shipments." Rather primly he added, "We carry more than adequate insurance at all times."

"Have all your coin shipments to Stella been stolen?" Longarm asked.

"Oh, no. We have been providing the Stella Mining Company with payroll for several years now. They do the bulk of their banking with us, you see. They ship processed ore. The smelter sends the raw gold to an agent in Chicago for sale in bulk. That firm deposits the profits in Stella's account here. We draw against that to provide their payroll coinage."

Longarm paused in thought. After a moment he said, "I'll want t' speak with your head teller and with this Davey person."

"Of course." Walters stood. He tugged his vest down where it had ridden up on his belly, then said, "Come with me, please."

Half an hour later Longarm left the First Commerce Bank and Trust, little wiser than when he arrived. He very seriously doubted that any of the employees there, from the bank president on down to Davey Fitzsimmon, had anything to do with the robberies.

One more Cheyenne bank to go, he thought. But he was beginning to doubt that he would learn anything of importance there, either. He wondered if there would be any point to a trip north to Miles City to speak with this Hal Tyler with the Bastrop Stage Line.

Chapter 11

"Hello, Marshal." Thomas Delancey smiled in welcome. "Do you have more questions for me?"

Longarm shook his head. "No. Matter o' fact, what I'm here for is transportation. I need t' get up to Miles City. Would Fremont offer somethin' going in that direction?"

"Easy enough done, Marshal. Our next coach north will leave at three tomorrow morning."

Longarm visibly winced. Delancey laughed and said, "I know. It isn't exactly convenient, is it. Will you be traveling with us?"

"I will."

"I'll make sure you have a seat." He laughed again and added, "Inside, so you can lean against something and go to sleep. No ticket necessary, of course."

"Thanks. Will I see you there tomorra morning when the damn thing loads?"

"Me?" Delancey feigned a look of shock. "Not me, Marshal. I intend to be sound asleep at that hour. But I might think about you tomorrow morning. Say, when I'm relaxing in my easy chair and enjoying that second cup of coffee."

"Thanks a lot," Longarm said drily.

"Can I check your bag on to Miles City then?" Delancey offered.

"That'd be good. Thanks."

Longarm wandered outside the Fremont Stage Company office and paused to light a cheroot. He really did not think there was much more he needed to do here in Cheyenne. And before he went up to Deadwood or to Lead he wanted to talk with that gent at the Bastrop line. Tyler, Delancey had said his name was. Harold Tyler? No, Hal. That was it. Hal Tyler. And he, too, was suffering losses from his shipments.

Coin headed to the same outfit in Deadwood? The content of those shipments and where they were consigned was one of the things he needed to learn.

Puffing on his cheroot, he ambled down the street and stepped inside the first storefront he came to that offered a whiff of beer and sawdust drifting out of the open doorway along with the sounds of friendly chatter and the clack of billiard balls.

"Mother, I'm home," he muttered under his breath as he pushed the batwings aside and entered the saloon.

Chapter 12

Longarm arrived in Miles City hot, weary, and covered with enough dust that he was fairly sure he could make a good crop if he planted potatoes in his crotch and armpits. He gave serious consideration to throwing himself, clothes and all, into the Yellowstone.

Instead he checked into the Debois Arms hotel and asked that a tub and hot water be brought up to his room. The request did not especially please the bellboy who would have to carry the water up two flights of stairs to reach him, but Longarm thought that was just too damn bad.

"An' I'll be wanting directions to a laundry and dry cleaners when I come back down."

"We can do the washing here, of course," the desk clerk said, "and Jimmy can take your dry cleaning. There is a Chinaman a block over who does a fine job. We always use him when a guest needs such service."

Longarm nodded and removed his tweed coat. "This is what I need cleaned with chemicals. Everything else can be washed, I reckon." He unloaded the pockets of the coat and handed it across the counter.

The clerk's nose wrinkled a bit in distaste, but he accepted the coat and, holding it with two fingers, laid it onto a chair. "We'll take care of it," he said.

"I'll pay for that separate," Longarm said. "I don't wanta put my personal stuff on the government voucher."

"Voucher? You didn't mention anything about a voucher, the clerk said, frowning.

"Gov'ment," Longarm said. "I'm a deputy marshal."

"Oh. I, uh, don't know if I can accept a voucher for payment. I have to talk with the owner about it."

Longarm smiled but with not the slightest hint of mirth or friendliness in the expression. "You can accept this one. Trust me 'bout that."

The desk clerk wilted under Longarm's gaze. "Yes, sir. But is it all right if I at least tell the owner?"

"Tell whoever you damn please but give me a room. An' that tub and hot water."

"Yes, sir."

Longarm trudged up the two flights of stairs to the top floor of the Debois, carrying his own carpetbag since Jimmy was occupied with the tweed coat, and found room number twelve right where the clerk had said it would be.

Longarm yawned his way into the room and looked for a place to sit down. There was no chair in the dingy little room and, filthy as he was, he did not want to sit on the clean bed. He settled for stripping off his clothes and sitting on the bottom end of the feather bed.

The bellhop was supposed to be on his way up with the tub and water so he did not want to go to sleep. He settled for cleaning his firearms, the Colt first. While the .45 was incapacitated with its component parts scattered onto the bedside table he placed the .41-caliber derringer where he could reach it.

He could not imagine there being a threat here in this hotel, but it would not be sensible to ignore the cautious habits of many years.

He was using a toothpick to drag the caked dust off the cylinder pawl when he heard a knock behind him.

"Come in," he said, concentrating on what he was doing. "Put the tub down over there an' get on with fetching the water, if you please."

He heard a laugh. A rather light and delicate laugh. And a decidedly female voice said, "I'm sorry. I don't have a tub with me."

Longarm stood and turned around before he remembered that he was naked.

Chapter 13

It was too late to do anything about his condition so he brazened it out, calmly setting the revolver frame down and leaning down to retrieve the balbriggans that he had dropped on top of the rest of his clothing. He picked up the soiled undergarment and held it strategically in front of his crotch.

He grinned and shrugged, then asked, "An' what can I do for you, ma'am?"

The lady stopped laughing long enough to say, "I came up here with one thing in mind but now that I see . . ." She cleared her throat and said, "I'm trying to remember what I wanted." She looked down toward Longarm's crotch again and rolled her eyes.

Mighty pretty eyes they were, he thought, as was the rest of her. She was blond with her hair done up in a tight, no-nonsense bun. She was short, probably not much more than five feet tall, and was so tightly laced into her corset that he could not guess at her figure. Her face, however, was more than pleasant to look at.

He guessed her age to be somewhere in her mid to late thirties.

"Oh, yes," she said. "Louis said you wanted to see me."

"I did?" Longarm said.

"That is what he told me. Something about taking a voucher to pay for the room?"

"Ah," he said. "That." He considered pulling on some clothes. But in order to do that he would have to drop the balbriggans and expose himself to her again, this time deliberately.

"You are a marshal?" she said.

"Deputy," he agreed. "Out o' Denver."

She giggled. "Do you always entertain ladies in this state of, um, dress?"

"When they're naked, too, I do," Longarm said.

That brought a laugh out of her. She started to say something but before she could get it out the bellboy arrived, finally, with the tub and a bucket of hot water.

"I have more water on the way, um, ah," he mumbled, glancing back and forth from his prim and proper boss to the naked guest and back again.

"Go get the rest of the water, Jimmy," the lady said.

"Yes, ma'am." Jimmy sounded grateful for a reason to flee. He turned and hustled out.

"Perhaps you need someone to pour the water and scrub your back," the lady said.

"Per'aps I do," Longarm agreed. "Know anyone who might apply for the job?"

"I just might."

"You realize that will purely scandalize poor Jimmy," Longarm said.

"If you have what I think I saw before you snatched up those underthings, I won't much care," the lady said.

"Are you getting fresh with me?" Longarm teased,

"Not at all," she answered, "merely applying for a job."

"Well, in that case all right. I reckon I could hire you on." He let the balbriggans fall away to his side, holding them with only one hand.

"Goodness," the woman said, licking her lips.

Longarm heard Jimmy on the stairs so he again covered himself.

The bellboy grunted and mumbled as he dragged the copper tub into the room and set the three buckets of steaming hot water beside it. "Is there anything else, ma'am?"

"No, Jimmy, that should be everything."

"Do you want me to, um . . . ?"

"No, Jimmy, you can leave now."

"Yes, ma'am." The young fellow turned and fled.

The lady stepped over to the door, closed it, and slid the bolt in place to lock it.

She was smiling when she turned back around.

Longarm tossed the balbriggans down on top of the rest of his soiled clothing.

Chapter 14

"Do you splash when you bathe?"

"Pardon me?" Longarm was confused by the question.

The lady smiled. "I am concerned that you might splash water on these clothes."

"Ah, yes. I just might splash you at that," Longarm agreed.

"It might be wise to remove them," she said. "Just in case."

"Very wise," he said.

She was still smiling when she began—very slowly—to remove her clothing, one piece at a time.

Her smile became even more broad when she saw Longarm's reaction. The taller his cock rose the broader her smile became.

She came closer and the smile disappeared. "You smell bad. Did you know that?"

"As I recall, ma'am, it's the reason I'm gonna take a bath." He grinned. "You were hired t' do a job, remember."

Her good humor returned. "Then step into the tub, sir,

and let's get you clean. Then we can, um, consider other things."

"As you wish." He got into the copper tub and hunkered down while the owner of the hotel poured hot water over him. When she emptied the first bucket she took a handful of soft soap and began to scrub him. She paid particular attention to his crotch, he noticed.

Not that he minded. Her touch was firm and more than pleasant, to the point that he damn near came when she washed his cock.

She also, he noticed, paid a great deal of attention to the crack of his ass. He could not help but wonder why.

When the lady was satisfied that he was thoroughly soaped and scrubbed she picked up another bucket of water and sluiced that over him. Once that bucket was empty she went to the third, soaked a washrag in that bucket and proceeded to finish rinsing him. With great, tender care. By the time she was done with that final process it was a wonder he did not squirt jism into her face when she leaned over him.

Smiling again she told him, "Stand up, please." She peeled his foreskin back, knelt, and took him into her mouth. That moist heat was more than he could ignore. He exploded into her mouth almost immediately.

"Good," she said, wiping her chin where a little of his juice had dribbled. "We got that out of the way. Now you should have a little staying power when you shove that beautiful thing into me."

And saying that, she took him by the balls and led him to the bed.

Led around by the . . . under the circumstances Longarm was willing to go along with the bossy broad.

Chapter 15

Longarm put his hand behind his head and lay back on the soft bed, the bossy lady asleep at his side. The woman was one hell of a wild ride, pumping as hard as he did or maybe more, time after time after . . . Yeah. A wild ride indeed.

He rolled onto his side and reached for a cheroot and match. He lighted the slim cigar and peered up toward the ceiling although not consciously seeing it.

"Let me have a drag on that," the lady said, waking but remaining completely still.

"You want a drag o' this smoke. Or of my cock?" he teased.

"Darlin', I'm too tired and sore right now to take any more of what you have. As it is it should be another four or five days before I feel right again."

"Look, if you're complaining . . ."

"Not that, dear. Never that. I just wish I had the stamina to go at it again with you." She sighed and sat up on the side of the bed. "Now, damnit, I have to get back to work. I have a hotel to run, after all, and you wouldn't believe the foolishness employees can get into if you don't watch them every second."

Longarm sat up, too, and eyed the now-cold water in the copper tub. He was sweaty enough that another wash would be in order. On the other hand he was tired enough that it could just wait until tomorrow. He smiled. Wouldn't Jimmy just love to carry more water for him?

The woman dressed quickly, bent to give him a quick kiss, and was gone, pulling the door closed behind her.

It occurred to Longarm that he had no idea what her name might be. Didn't all that much care, really. What he knew about her was that she gave a great fuck. What more did a man really need to know about a woman beyond that?

He felt of the water in the tub—cold, as he expected—but drenched a washrag anyway and wiped himself off with it, then dressed in clean clothing from the carpetbag. He finished cleaning and assembling the .45 and cleaned the derringer next, although it had been in his pocket protected from the dust and really did not need much attention.

Finally he stamped into his boots, grabbed his Stetson, and went downstairs in search of supper. Funny how he had worked up such an appetite.

Chapter 16

After all that healthy exercise Longarm was in the mood for something more substantial than a greasy-spoon meal so he walked past two seedy cafés until he found a proper restaurant. The place had curtains at the windows. More important, the smells drifting through the open doorway got his mouth to watering and his belly to rumbling. He headed inside and even removed his Stetson, something he did not always do.

"Sit wherever you like," a tall, cadaverously thin man greeted him. The fellow was wearing an apron and held a towel in one hand and a printed menu in the other.

Longarm chose a table that put his back to the wall and gave him a view of the front door. He was not expecting trouble. But then trouble comes at its own pace, whether a man is ready for it or not; it is best to stay ready for it, Longarm had found.

"We're out of the baked chicken," the waiter said, handing him the menu. "Otherwise you can order whatever you see there."

Longarm barely glanced at the menu. "Roast buff'lo

hump," he said, "with the mashed taters an' gravy. Peas."
He paused. "An' a big slab o' apple pie t' pack it all down."

"Very good, sir." The waiter retrieved the menu and
disappeared into the back of the place. He returned almost
instantly with a carafe and poured Longarm a cup of
steaming hot coffee. The aroma coming off the cup was
tantalizing.

He picked the cup up and was about to dip his mustache into the richly black fluid when a lady on the other
side of the room cried out. Longarm looked up in time to
see the gentleman with her reach out and grab her by the
arm, taking a firm hold and twisting her arm cruelly.

The woman was a plump matron, nicely dressed. Her
companion was middle-aged and burly, wearing a tweed
suit and string tie. The fellow had red hair and was beginning to go bald, a palm-sized patch of bare skin appear-
ing on the back of his head.

"Please, Daniel," she pleaded. "Don't."

Daniel leaned forward and growled something that
Longarm could not hear. Then he slapped the lady. Hard.

Longarm was out of his chair before he consciously
realized it. He took three long strides and ended up standing over the pair.

The big man looked up, his face red with fury. "What
the fuck do you want, mister? Butt out. This ain't any of
your business."

"You're right," Longarm said.

Then slapped the son of a bitch. Hard.

The man's head was driven to the side. Hard.

His neck swelled up like a bull buffalo's and he came
out of his chair. Hard.

Longarm's right fist met the charge. Hard.

The man screamed. More with rage and anger than
in pain.

Longarm hit him again, this time in the belly.

The big man doubled over and sagged to a knee. He stayed there for only a moment, then straightened with a roar and again tried to put Longarm down.

His effort was thwarted by a combination of punches as Longarm flashed a combination of lefts and rights that tattooed the man's nose and jaw, splitting his upper lip and smashing his nose flat.

Blood sprayed onto the white tablecloth and the man staggered. Longarm hit him again. And twice more. He went down again, this time onto both knees. And this time he stayed down, his head drooping, blood dripping from nose and mouth.

"I'll have . . . the law . . . on you . . . you son of a . . . bitch," he breathed, his voice hollow because of the blood that blocked his nose.

"You do that," Longarm snarled. He turned toward the lady.

Who slapped him across the face. Hard.

"Wha . . . ?"

"Leave my husband alone, you big ape," she yelled.

The woman threw herself down beside her kneeling, reeling husband and cradled his bloody head in her arms. "What did that man do to you, sweetie?" she crooned. "Are you all right? Don't worry, dearest. I'll take care of you. It will be just fine now." She rocked him back and forth like a little baby.

Longarm shook his head in amazement, then turned and went back to his own table, marveling at human foolishness.

"Are you ready for your supper now, sir?" the waiter asked, unperturbed by the outburst in his dining room.

"I am," Longarm said as he once again slipped in behind the table and sat surveying the room.

Chapter 17

"There, Donald. That's him." It was the big man, back again, this time with his face washed clean—come tomorrow morning it would be swollen and discolored—and with another man beside him. He was pointing an accusing finger at Longarm. There was no sign of the abused wife.

The Donald he was speaking to was slender, with graying dark blond hair. Donald wore a broadcloth suit. He did not have a tie but he did wear a revolver holster showing beneath the hem of the suit coat. He also had a round badge pinned prominently on the lapel of the coat.

"The son of a bitch assaulted me, Donald. I'll press charges, you can be sure of that." His voice was pitched loud enough to carry throughout the restaurant.

Heads turned. For the second time. The same diners witnessed the fight—what little there was of it—not twenty minutes earlier. Now they looked to see what would happen to the stranger once the law got hold of him.

Donald approached Longarm warily, one hand already draped over the butt of his Colt, but the gun remaining in the leather.

"I was gonna look you up come mornin'," Longarm
drawled, "but I reckon now is as good a time as any."

"If you want to press charges . . ."

"Aw, no need for that," Longarm said, glancing past
Donald to the big man, who now was looking very pleased
with himself.

"Mr. Connerly here is—"

"Is an asshole," Longarm interrupted. "Mind if I reach
inta my pocket for something, Donald?"

"Fine, but do it slowly, please."

Longarm kept his hand well clear of the Colt that rode
at his waist, instead dipping his fingers into the inside
pocket of his coat and retrieving his wallet. He pulled it
out and flipped it open so Donald could see the badge
that was pinned inside.

"Oh. You are . . ."

"Deputy U.S. Marshal Custis Long, out o' Denver."

"You're one of Billy Vail's deputies? Lord, I've known
Billy for years and years. Used to know him down in
Texas when he was a ranger and I was just starting out
with the Austin police department."

Longarm nodded.

"Custis Long, you said?"

He nodded again.

"You're the one they call Longarm."

Another nod.

Donald turned to the aggrieved local citizen. "Don't
worry, Charles. I'll take care of this. Go on about your
business now. I have it under control."

"If you're sure . . ."

"I am. Go on now."

The big fellow huffed and rolled his shoulders but he
turned away, probably more than happy to let someone
else tangle with the situation, and left the restaurant. The

tension that had been in the room since his return evaporated and folks went back to their suppers. Donald reached for the back of the chair opposite Longarm's and said, "Mind if I sit?"

"Please," Longarm said. "I'm just fixin' to have some deep-dish apple pie that if it's good as it looks, well . . ." He rolled his eyes and grinned. "Join me?"

"Don't mind if I do," Donald said. He turned before he sat and said, "I'll have coffee, Dennis, and some of that pie." He pulled the chair out and sat down, reaching a hand across the table to shake with Longarm on his way down. "Pleased to meet you, Long. I've heard good things about you."

"Thanks. And you are . . . ?"

"Donald Hauser. I'm town marshal, chief deputy, and general dogsbody hereabouts."

"My pleasure, Don. I'll tell Billy where I seen you."

"Do that, please. What brings you up this way, Longarm?"

Dennis arrived with two generous slabs of pie, a cup of coffee for Hauser, and a refill for Longarm.

Longarm quickly filled the local man in on his problem, concluding with, "I been hoping you could give me something t' go on 'bout these holdups. I know most of 'em originated, the coaches that is, down in Cheyenne, but at least some were rolling out o' Miles City. I'm told a gent name of Hal Tyler with the Bastrop stage line would be able to give me the details up here."

"Not anymore he can't," Hauser said. "Hal quit his job with Bastrop and pulled stakes. Said he was going to try his luck in San Francisco or some such warmer place."

Longarm laughed. "You ever been to San Fran?"

Hauser shook his head. "No, never."

"Neither has Tyler."

"Why would you say that?"

"If he thinks San Francisco is warmer, he hasn't."

"Cold place?"

"Terrible. Damn wind there cuts bone deep. It's a diff'rent sort o' cold from up here. Anyway I was hopin' to talk to the man 'bout these robberies."

"The way I understand it," Hauser said, "he didn't know much he could have told you about them. The way it worked, whenever an outfit in Deadwood wanted money shipped to them they wired ahead for it. They had some sort of code worked out between the bank and this mining company so nobody except the folks who needed to know could figure it out. Tyler and me sat down and talked it over plenty, but we neither one of us could see where anyone at this end tipped the robbers to the shipment."

"Do you know where the money was consigned?" Longarm asked.

"Of course," Hauser said with a nod. "They were going . . . let me see if I can remember. One was going to the Lady Blue mine. Another was a shipment to the Deadwood bank . . . I forget the exact name of it . . . some sort of transfer between sister banks, as I understand it."

"Going to different places," Longarm mused aloud, "with different people involved each time."

"That would be about right," Hauser said. "How does that stack up with the Cheyenne experience?"

"Much the same," Longarm admitted. "It don't give us much to work from."

Hauser grunted. "That's likely the exact same way the robbers want you to see it. Which, come to think of it, raised the question about why you federal boys are looking into it. I thought this was strictly territorial jurisdiction."

Longarm explained about mail clerk Clarence Osgood and the mail being sent via strongbox.

"Smart thinking," Hauser agreed, digging into his pie.

Longarm had almost forgotten about dessert. The pie, when he got to it, was as good as anything he had had in a very long while, if ever.

"Where will you go from here?" Hauser asked.

"Deadwood, I reckon. Unless you got a better idea." He frowned. "I sure don't." He finished the last of his pie and held his empty cup high to call for a refill.

"If I could think of anything, I would damn sure tell you," Hauser said. "But I can't."

"Yeah. Me, neither." He sighed. "But, Lordy, I do hate for a robber gang like that t' keep getting away with what they been doing." He smiled. "Maybe if I'm lucky they'll hit the stage I take down to Deadwood. That will put paid to the sons o' bitches."

"I sort of hate to hope that the stage is held up again," Hauser said with a grin, "but this time I will." He shoved back from the table and stood. "Thanks for the dessert."

"Hey, wait. Aren't you gonna arrest me for assaulting that stupid son of a bitch in here?"

Hauser just laughed and turned away.

"Reckon not," Longarm mumbled under his breath as he reached for his coffee cup. Damn, but that was a fine meal. And on the heels of an even more fine fuck. He wondered what the lady hotelkeeper would be doing for the rest of the evening, because after that good meal and a little time to recuperate, he was ready to go at her again.

Chapter 18

He never got an opportunity to bang the lady hotelkeeper another time. When he got back to the Debois Arms the woman acted like she had never before seen him, much less wallowed around with him making the beast with two backs. If anything she acted cold and aloof from him.

But he did find out from the desk clerk that her name was Pansy Dantzler and she owned not only the Debois but several other businesses in Miles City as well.

Screwing Pansy again being out of the question, Longarm settled for a few shots of rye whiskey at a nearby saloon, then turned in and got a good night's sleep.

Morning found him unusually well rested—sleep being the aftermath of a good fuck—and searching for the Bastrop office, which he found at the east end of town.

"No, sir, I don't know much about those robberies," the current station chief told him. "I was brought in from Lewistown to take over when Hal left. Heard about them, of course. We don't get so very many robberies now that the boom has died down, so they were the talk of the company when they happened. I wish I could help you."

"You can," Longarm told him.

"Anything I can do, just name it."

"I need transportation down to Deadwood," Longarm said. "Lead, too, I suppose."

The man's expression brightened. "Now that I can do for you. We have a coach leaving this afternoon at two. It goes through Belle Fourche and Lead then back up the gulch to Deadwood."

"Regular run?" Longarm asked.

The helpful gent nodded. "Twice a week, regular as a clock."

"Lucky timing," Longarm said. He grinned and added, "Saves my butt from having to make the ride on a rented horse, an' you know how bad some o' them can be. Count me in for a seat on that two o'clock stage, please."

"It will be my pleasure, Marshal."

Longarm turned away, then had another thought and turned back. "Will you by any chance be carrying a bank transfer or a payroll for the Lady Blue?"

"Not that I know of," the station chief said, "but then we never know ahead of time, not until the very last moment."

"If your bank here does consign a shipment with you today, let me know when I come to board, will you?"

"Count on it, Marshal."

Longarm went back to the hotel to retrieve the clothes he had worn up from Cheyenne—they had been at the dry cleaners . . . and damn sure needed cleaning—and pack ready for the next leg of his journey.

While he was in his room packing, Pansy Dantzler showed up, wanting another wrestling match.

"No, thanks," Longarm told her, offering no explanations to soften the rejection. He got a hell of a kick out of the look on the woman's face when he turned her down. Very likely it was an experience she never in her life had before. And it was about damn time that she did, he thought. She was good in bed, there was no doubt about that, but she was full of herself and needed to be taken down a peg.

And anyway he was busy.

He finished packing, carried his carpetbag over to the Bastrop office to be put aboard the two o'clock stage, bought a pint of rye to fortify himself on the road, and went to have some lunch before the trip.

Chapter 19

Longarm was slumped in the corner of the rear seat on a Concord stage that was much larger than was necessary, at least for this run. In front of him, on the rear-facing bench, were two whores whose perfume could not completely mask the fact that they needed to bathe. Beside him dozed a drummer who sold hardware. The middle bench was empty.

The coach rocked and swayed outrageously on the leather suspension straps that served as springs. The motion was very similar to that of a boat in choppy water, so much so that one of the whores had become seasick and puked out the window.

Longarm yawned and stretched. He gave some thought to the question of should he try to sleep. Or not bother trying.

"Whoa. Whoa, you sons o' bitches," the driver called from his box high above the four-up out front.

Must be some obstruction on the road, Longarm assumed, because they were not due into Belle Fourche

for—he pulled his Ingersoll out and checked the time—
not for another three quarters of an hour or more.

The coach came to a stop, rocking back and forth on
the suspension. The driver called out, "We have a box here
but it's empty. That's why I don't got no shotgun messen-
ger, mister."

Longarm's interest quickened. They were being
robbed? Well, it was what he had been hoping for. But it
surprised him nonetheless.

"Toss it down," another voice came from in front of
the stage.

"Suit yourself," the driver responded, "but I'm tellin'
you there ain't nothing in it."

There was a slight pause, then the dull thump of something heavy—the strongbox, no doubt—hitting the road.

"Now the passengers," the distant voice demanded.
"Get 'em out."

"Fuck you. Get them out yourself," the driver said.

"Mind your tongue, old man, or I'll blow you off that
high horse you're riding."

The driver shut up after that and a moment later a man
wearing an oversized linen duster and a flour-sack mask
over his head appeared beside the coach.

"Everybody out," he ordered. "Hands high. Empty
your pockets."

Longarm pushed ahead of the hardware drummer to
reach the door first. He motioned for the two whores to
get down onto the floor.

"Hurry up. We ain't got all day."

"We," the highwayman said. So he had at least one
partner out there out of Longarm's line of sight.

"Come on now."

Longarm palmed his .45 and pushed the coach door
open.

Chapter 20

"You're under arrest," he said as he stepped out of the Concord.

The robber jerked—startled, no doubt, although Longarm could not see his facial expression beneath that hood—and brought the muzzle of his revolver around toward Longarm. Any self-respecting robber would have been aiming toward the coach to begin with, of course.

Then he made his second mistake. And by far his worse one. He cocked his piece—again it rightly should have been ready to fire to start with—and tried to shoot Custis Long in the face.

Before the man could trigger his Smith & Wesson Schofield, Longarm put a bullet in his chest and another in the belly. The first slug knocked him back a step. The second doubled him over with a cry of pain.

"You didn't . . . you didn't have to . . ."

By that time Longarm was on the ground in a crouch, looking around for the others.

He saw no one.

"You up there. Jehu," he called up to the driver. "D'you see any more of 'em?"

The pale, obviously frightened stagecoach driver crawled up from the floor of his driving box and peered over the side.

"I asked you . . ."

"I heard you, mister. Jesus. That was scary. Fourteen years I been driving for Bastrop and this is the first time I ever been held up. I didn't like it, not one bit."

"Mister, do you see any more of them?" Longarm repeated.

The driver finally paid attention to the question. He shuddered, shaken badly, but said, "No, I only seen the one."

Longarm frowned. This was *almost* the way they said the robbers worked. Almost. Not quite.

The way he understood it there should have been at least one more robber there to back up the first one. And the robbers were said to never speak. Never. They just gestured with the muzzles of their shotguns.

Which was another thing. This guy had a revolver but no shotgun.

Still, the duster was correct as was the flour-sack hood. And the son of a bitch had indeed tried to hold up the coach. A coach, come to think of it, with an empty strongbox.

That was another thing, Longarm was thinking as he carefully shucked the empty brass out of his Colt and reloaded with fresh cartridges from his coat pocket. Always before the robbers seemed to know in advance that the shipment included cash. Not this time.

"Are you sure you don't see no others?" he called up to the driver.

"Mister, if I seen any more of 'em I wouldn't be setting up here in plain sight. I'd still be down in my box."

Longarm grunted. He shoved his Colt back into the leather, but warily. He was not yet satisfied that the robber had been alone.

"Come on down an' help me," he told the driver.

"What for?"

"'Cause we got to take care of this fellow."

"You mean maybe he isn't dead?"

"Oh, I'm pretty sure he's dead. But we can't leave him laying here. I want t' pick him up an' haul him into Belle Fourche."

"You're gonna get blood all inside my coach. The section boss will be pissed."

"We can put him in the luggage boot. But we got to carry him in with us. Now come on down an' help me."

With obvious distaste for the chore, the jehu set his brake and came down off the box.

Longarm knelt beside the dead robber and pulled the hood off, exposing a seedy-looking middle-aged man who had not shaved in days and whose hollowed cheeks suggested he might not have eaten in some time, either.

"Know him?" he asked the driver when the man joined him.

The jehu shook his head. "Never saw him before. Nor any posters on him, neither."

Longarm checked the man's pockets but found nothing more interesting than a snot-stiff bandana and a rusty barlow knife. He retrieved the Schofield from where it had fallen and stuffed it behind the dead man's belt. There was no holster for it. Apparently the man had not been in the habit of carrying a revolver or just chose to carry it in his waistband. He had no spare ammunition for the pistol.

Every way he looked at it, Longarm thought, this seemed an amateur attempt at highway robbery. It just did not fit with all the things he had heard about this rob-ber gang.

"You got 'im, Marshal. You put an end to our string of holdups," the driver said.

By then the other passengers were out of the coach and coming timidly forward to gather over the dead rob-ber and stare down at him. It was an impulse Longarm had never understood but one that was common.

"Come on you," he said to the drummer. "The three of us can lift this guy easy enough. We'll put him in the luggage boot an' carry him to town with us."

One of the whores, the one who had gotten seasick earlier in the trip, bent down and wet a forefinger in the poor son of a bitch's blood.

"Why'd you do that?" Longarm asked her.

The chippy shrugged. "I dunno, I just . . . I dunno."

Longarm and the other two men made easy work of picking the robber up and carrying him to the coach. They transferred all the baggage to the roof of the coach and the driver secured the leather luggage boot with the corpse inside.

"Everybody back aboard now," the jehu called. "We'll be late as it is so let's not make this any worse than it's gotta be."

Longarm helped the two women into the coach, stood aside for the salesman to board and then climbed inside himself. Up on the driving box the jehu took up his lines and snapped his whip above the ears of his leaders. The Bastrop coach lurched into motion and they were once more rolling toward Belly Fourche.

Longarm sat slouched in his corner again but this time he was not dozing. This time he was pondering, and what he kept coming back to was that he indeed had stopped a robbery. But he more than likely had not stopped the robbers he had come here to find.

Chapter 21

"Marshal, I'm god-awful sorry but I'm already behind schedule. You got to do what you got to do, but so do I. And what I got to do is get on with my route. You can catch the next coach through. That's all there is to it."

"When is that?" Longarm asked. They were stopped outside the barbershop in Belle Fourche, where they had just unloaded the body of the dead highwayman for the barber, who also served as the town's undertaker, to undertake.

"It ain't but three days, Marshal. That's our next outfit down."

Longarm grunted. Three days in Belle Fourche was not exactly what he had planned. But he did want to speak with the local marshal and, if possible, the county sheriff as well. One of them might know more about the robbers. The successful ones, that is, not the poor dead son of a bitch laid out on the undertaker's slab now.

"Fine then. Hand me down my carpetbag."

The driver crawled onto the roof of his coach. He

retrieved the bag in question and handed it down to Longarm. Then the man took up his driving lines and put the coach into motion again. He looked pleased to be leaving Custis Long behind.

The barber was standing on the boardwalk behind him. "Mind if I leave my bag with you till I figure out what I'm doin' tonight?" Longarm asked.

"You can leave the bag, Marshal, but who'll be paying for the laying out and the burying?"

"You'll have t' talk with your sheriff 'bout that, I'd think," Longarm said. "I'd expect the county t' pay, but that ain't up to me."

The barber, a beefy man with thinning hair, reached up to scratch his nose. Longarm noticed that his hands were bloody almost up to the elbows. Very likely, Longarm thought, the fellow had already dug the bullets out of the robber's body. He probably would sell those to someone as souvenirs. Likely would have photographs taken, too. He might have to split those profits with the photographer but the bullets and anything else he could scavenge off—or out of—the body would be his alone. Longarm always found undertaking to be a damned strange business. Necessary, though.

Longarm set his bag inside the barbershop doorway and thanked the barber for the courtesy, then asked, "Where can I find your sheriff?"

"His office is over in the county courthouse. That's it over there." The man pointed toward a sprawling single-story structure two blocks over. "Marshal Bennett is across the street in the city hall. You can't see it from here but there's a sign. The sheriff is Ed Hochavar."

"Bennett," Longarm repeated, "an' Hochavar. All right, thanks."

"Ask them who's gonna pay," the barber said.

"I'll do that, you bet," Longarm responded, not meaning a word of it. "Oh, one more thing. Where's the telegraph office here?"

"That would be in the post office. It's right around the corner from the courthouse."

"You been a big help. Thanks." Longarm touched the brim of his Stetson, then turned and headed down the street in the direction of the local government buildings.

He undoubtedly would be asked to fill out some paperwork about the dead man. And if he was going to be stuck here for three days he might as well send a wire to Billy Vail informing the boss about the state of his investigation. Such as it was.

Chapter 22

Ed Hochavar was a big man with a big belly. He was getting on in years, late fifties or early sixties, Longarm guessed. That was old for a lawman. The sheriff was obviously liked by the local citizens, though, or they would not keep voting him into office.

When Longarm introduced himself, Hochavar extended a welcoming hand and said, "You're the deputy who killed Tom Bowen this morning, right?"

"Bowen," Longarm said. "I didn't know the man's name."

"Tom has . . . had, I should say . . . a hardscrabble farm north of town. Dumb son of a bitch left a widow and half a dozen kids out there. I've already sent a man to tell Jeanine about her husband." He shook his head. "Tony Conseca over at the barber shop is going to be pretty pissed off. Jeanine won't be able to pay for the burying."

"What about the county?" Longarm asked.

Hochavar shrugged. "Wasn't our kill nor capture so I don't see as how the county should be on the hook for it.

I suppose we'll just have to pass the hat around our saloons and maybe Sunday morning at church services. We'll manage, of course. Folks always do, one way or another."

"I can kick in a little, too," Longarm offered.

"That's good of you, Deputy."

"T' tell the truth though, Sheriff, Bowen isn't why I wanted t' talk to you."

Hochavar's eyebrows went up. "Oh?"

"What I'm here about, sheriff, is your successful highway robbers. We both know that Bowen didn't pull those jobs. I'd like you t' tell me whatever you know about them."

"I know they were committed across the line into Montana Territory. Out of my jurisdiction, you know."

"Of course. Right now I'm looking for information, that's all."

Hochavar harrumphed and reached into a pocket for a meerschaum pipe that had passed through the golden color to a dark, glossy brown. "No offense taken, young fellow. I just want to be clear about this."

"I assume you've spoken with the drivers and maybe some passengers who were robbed."

"Now that's one thing," the sheriff said. "They all say the same. The robbers were quiet. Not a peep out of them during the holdups. And the passengers weren't bothered. All they wanted was the cash box. And every time those boxes were full of currency and coin. They don't hit every shipment of cash but whenever they hit there was plenty of cash in those boxes to be had."

"Have details of the robberies been made public?" Longarm asked.

Hochavar nodded. "Of course. We don't have a newspaper of our own, but there are papers in Lead and

Deadwood and Miles City, too. We get all of them and they all had stories in them about the robberies."

"Including the story by Jennifer Wiley? She's the English-woman who . . ."

Hochavar waved his hand dismissively. "Oh, I know Jen, all right, but she's no more an Englishwoman than I am. She came out here as kitchen help in Lord Banfield's hunting party. Her real name is Jennifer Vaughn and she is from the Bowery in New York City. Yeah, I know Jen, all right."

"Is she still here? Can I interview her?"

"Sorry. She's long gone. I don't even know if she went back East or traveled on to California like she talked of doing."

"Was she telling the truth in that article?" Longarm asked.

"Who knows. It could be, I suppose," Hochavar said, "but I wouldn't bank on it. She liked a tall tale as well as anybody." The sheriff winked. "Liked her whiskey as good as anybody, too. Could have been whiskey talking in that story. Or she could have stumbled into something when she was passing herself off as a newspaperwoman. Which is what she wanted to be. The chance to travel and to see strange sights is probably why she took that job to begin with. That and to escape from the Bowery. She never admitted to me what she had done back there but I got the idea that it was something pretty bad."

"How'd you come to know her?" Longarm asked.

The sheriff laughed. "Jen acted almost like a man. Her and me played cards together and drank some together. She isn't a bad-looking girl and I think she liked me because I wasn't always trying to get in her knickers the way most of the fellows did. With me it was just the cards and the liquor. And talk. Jen likes to talk."

"But she's gone now?"

Hochavar nodded. "Weeks ago."

"Damn. I'd hoped to talk to her," Longarm said.

"Sorry."

"In your honest opinion, was she telling the truth in that article?"

"I just don't know, Long. I just can't help you there."

"One more thing, Sheriff." Longarm grinned. "Is there a decent hotel in town? It looks like I'll be here for a few days until the next coach comes through."

"Sure thing. You just go three blocks that way and . . ."

Chapter 23

It was a hotel, all right. As for how good a hotel it was, well, Longarm was reserving judgment about that. It seemed a little on the seedy side but he could have been wrong about that. And it did have a bed and a door that could be bolted shut. Beyond that it did not much matter.

He looked through his carpetbag to make sure there was nothing contained in it that could not be easily replaced—just in case the mice in the hotel had sticky fingers—and deposited the bag underneath the rumpled bed, the appearance of which made him suspect that the sheets were not changed very often.

For whatever it was worth he locked the hotel room door behind him—the lock could be jimmied with a butter knife—and went downstairs.

"Where can I find a good café?" he asked the desk man.

"There's a café in the next block over," the fellow told him. Then he grinned and added, "Or there's a *good* café in the next block after that one. Dud's place. And it would be a kindness if you'd mention that I sent you."

"Dud?"

"Short for Dudley."

"Thanks." He left the hotel and went to the closer café, not the one that would give a kickback to the hotel clerk, figuring that his recommendation had nothing to do with the quality of either place.

The meal he got there was tasty and inexpensive and the place was clean. Longarm figured a fellow couldn't ask for much better than that. Not in a town he was just passing through. He ate, paid, and grabbed a toothpick on his way out the door.

As he was passing a store on his way back to the hotel he heard a loud crash and an even louder yelp of "damn you, Larry" coming from inside. The voice was a woman's, and she sounded both angry and scared.

On an impulse Longarm turned and stepped inside.

The store proved to deal in ladies' ready-to-wear, hats and dresses and unmentionables. Toward the back of the display space a woman was trying to fend off a tall, rangy man with blond hair and a mustache so pale it was difficult to see. The man wore a boiled shirt but no collar. He had garters on his sleeves.

The woman was a good foot shorter than the man and he probably outweighed her by fifty pounds. She was backed into a corner, spitting and clawing but quite obviously was losing this battle.

It hardly seemed a fair contest so Longarm crossed the small room and politely tapped the gent on his shoulder.

The fellow did not respond to the first light tap so Longarm tried again. Harder.

And when that did not work he grabbed the fellow by the arm and yanked him around so the two were face-to-face.

"Par'n me, ma'am," Longarm said with a nod toward the lady.

Then he punched the man in the face.

That got his attention just fine.

The man let go of the woman and threw a quick left at Longarm.

Longarm swayed aside just enough to let the punch fly harmlessly past then dug a hard blow to the fellow's ribs.

Had his attention? And then some. The man turned pale with pain but he was game. He moved in closer to Longarm and threw a left, which Longarm ducked, and followed it with a sharp right that connected with Longarm's jaw.

Longarm's face went numb. And he was pissed. He pummeled the SOB with a flurry of lefts and rights and lefts again.

With his back against the wall there was nowhere for the man to retreat toward. He tried to duck but to no avail. Within seconds his face was running with blood from a split lip and a smashed nose. A cut over his right eye must have nearly blinded him because he was no longer able to see to even try to block Longarm's rain of fists.

"Enough!" he cried out, leaning back against the wall with his forearms guarding his battered face. "Enough."

Longarm stopped punching, and the man ducked between Longarm and the woman to make his escape at a run, his shoe soles pounding across the floor. He slammed the shop door so hard it was a wonder he did not break the glass.

"Are you all right?"

Longarm looked down to see a very pretty, middle-aged woman. Until then he had paid little attention to her, being somewhat busy elsewhere.

She was small and lightly built. She had dark hair except for a few strands of gray showing at her temples. Her hair was pulled back in a severe bun. She wore a starched white shirtwaist and a black skirt.

She reached up and touched his cheek. He winced. He really had not realized that he was hit that hard in that brief dustup.

"You're hurt," she said.

Longarm harrumphed. "Not half as bad as that son of a . . . uh, as that other fella."

The woman laughed. "The son of a bitch you refer to is my ex-husband, Larry." She had a good laugh, light and delicate and pleasing to the ear. "I have to agree that he got the worse of the bargain. Come into the back with me for a minute. I have some water there. I'll bathe that cut."

"Cut?"

"It's just a little one, but we wouldn't want it to get infected, would we?"

"No, uh, we wouldn't want that."

Smiling, she went to the front door and threw the bolt to lock it, then fetched a CLOSED sign from behind a rack of hats and set that in the window. Then she returned to Longarm and took him by the hand.

Chapter 24

The back room was obviously a storeroom, but she had a bed there, too. A double bed, curtained off from the storage part of the room. The little woman held out her hand to shake and introduced herself. "My name is Angela Morris." She grinned. "But I am no angel."

Longarm completed his side of the introduction.

"A marshal," she said. "I hope you are no angel, either, Marshal Long."

"Now that is one thing I never been accused of, Miss Morris."

"Please call me Angela."

"All right. Angela it is."

She gave him an impish smile. "And now, Marshal, you know why my husband left me."

"I do?"

"Yes. It is because I have this insatiable desire to fuck every man I meet." She tilted her head to the side and smiled again. "Right now, for instance. Do you mind?"

"Are you serious?"

"Very." She began removing her clothes, the shirtwaist first, then her skirt and the blouse.

"Reckon," he said, "I don't mind."

Angela Morris was small, with a compact body. Thin legs. Tiny tits that lay flat against her chest. Dark nipples that stood erect and proud. A bushy vee of hair at her crotch.

"Hurry," she whispered, her voice low and throaty now. "Hurry, please. I need it. Please."

Longarm hurried. It would have been rude to turn away now. He stripped as quickly as he could, his cock standing tall and eager.

Angela grabbed his hand and pulled him to the bed. She lay down, spreading herself open to him.

Longarm practically threw himself onto her. And into her.

She was already wet in anticipation of what was to come. "All of it. Yes. Give it to me."

Incredibly, she began to shudder in a hard climax almost before he could fill her. She was as quick to come as he could ever recall knowing, and she continued to come time after time while he stroked into her and built to his own powerful climax.

When he tried to roll off of her, thinking his weight might be too much for her small frame, Angela stopped him, wrapping her arms around him and asked, "Stay. Please. I love to feel you inside of me, so big and warm and nice. You fill me. Not every man can do that."

He stayed. He kissed her, her tongue probing inside his mouth. After a moment he began to grow hard again and the stroking resumed, more slowly this time though. Angela closed her eyes and lifted her hips to him, timing her thrusts to his. She began to come again, spasming time after time.

"Nice," he said.

Eventually—he had no idea how much time might have passed—she said, "We have to stop now." She laughed. "I'm too sore to go any longer. I'm sorry."

The truth was that he was not a bit sorry. He was damn near worn out by so much of a good thing.

Angela got a hand towel and wiped him off, then cleaned herself while Longarm dressed.

"Will I see you again?" she asked.

He shrugged. "That depends on things that ain't all in my control."

"Come by if you find the time," she offered. "My door is always open." She laughed and cupped her pussy in one hand. "So are other things, too."

Longarm put on his hat and started for the door.

"One more thing," Angela said.

He stopped, his hand on the doorknob.

"It's my husband. Watch out for him. Larry is . . . excitable. And a sneak. So be careful."

"Thanks." He let himself out the door. Angela was naked and in no condition to be seen. He would have locked it behind him except he did not have a key, so he settled for leaving the CLOSED sign in the window and making sure the door was latched behind him when he left.

Chapter 25

The sun was disappearing somewhere beyond the buildings on the other side of the street when Longarm left
Angela's Ladieswear. He had already had his supper earlier but he was feeling a mite puckish after his wrestling
match with Angela Morris. And anyway he had no desire
to spend the evening in that drab little hotel room.

He checked the lamps that were beginning to show
up and down the street and decided on a saloon that was
close to the center of town. His experience was that such
places generally had a quiet clientele. That would suit
him just fine for this evening.

As he had hoped the place was, if not silent, at least
calm when he entered. There were a good many customers, most of them seated at the several round tables that
dotted the sawdust.

Another good sign was that there were no whores in
the place. It was obviously a saloon where the local gents
came to drink and socialize and unwind after their days
of doing whatever it was that they did to make a living.

Longarm nodded to the barkeep and placed a quarter

on the bar. "Rye whiskey an' a beer chaser," he said. He examined the free lunch spread and helped himself to a pickled egg.

"Coming right up, friend."

The rye was of an excellent quality, and the beer had a crisp, clean flavor. Longarm saluted the bartender with his glass.

"Excuse me, mister."

Longarm turned to see a gentleman in sleeve garters and a bowler hat. "Yes?"

"I don't know if you play poker, but we're looking for a fourth hand at our table. It's just casual play. Low stakes, if that makes a difference. We'd be pleased if you'd join us."

Longarm smiled. "Sir, you just made my evenin'. I'd be right happy t' join you."

He spent the next very pleasant hours playing stud poker and came away about a dollar and a half down. Longarm considered it money well spent for a thoroughly enjoyable evening.

About ten o'clock the game broke up, the other gents heading home to their families. Longarm stayed for a nightcap, then tipped the bartender a half dollar and headed back toward the hotel.

Chapter 26

Come morning Longarm was lazy; he stayed in bed a good half hour past dawn. Then he got up, dressed, and went in search of first a breakfast and then a shave. Both were more than satisfactory. The barber in particular had a nice touch, his razor featherlight on the skin but leaving not a hint of beard behind. Longarm was so pleased with his shave that he tipped the man a dime.

Done with the morning necessities, he looked up Town Marshal John Bennett—tall, young, and eager—but learned nothing new about the robberies. From there he found the Bastrop office and spoke with the line's agent.

Lew Arnold was a shopkeeper who contracted with Bastrop to handle their freight and ticketing rather than being employed by the line full time. He was aware of the robberies, of course, but could add nothing to what Longarm already knew.

"In my opinion, Marshal," Arnold said, "Tom Bowen was not the man who pulled those other robberies."

"I agree," Longarm told him.

Arnold nodded toward the front door of his saddlery

and harness shop. "In case you're interested, I saw Jeanine go past a couple minutes ago. Looked like she was headed for Bix Dooley's place."

"And Dooley would be . . . ?"

"Our barber. He has . . ."

"The body. Right," Longarm said. "I helped drop him off the stagecoach yesterday."

Considering that he was the person who shot her husband down, Widow Bowen might not welcome a sympathy call from Custis Long. Still, he felt he owed it to the lady to pay his respects. He thanked Lew Arnold and headed back to the barbershop he had left just a couple of hours earlier.

The street in front of the barbershop had been empty when Longarm was there before, Belle Fourche not being so large that men could not walk in for their morning shaves. Now there was a buckboard parked there, drawn by a pair of undersized Spanish mules.

Longarm paused to scratch the mules under their jaws—he liked mules and anyway was in no hurry to confront Jeanine Bowen—then squared shoulders and marched inside.

The only person he saw inside was a customer who was already in the chair, lathered and covered with an apron.

"Where's Dooley?" Longarm asked.

The customer pointed toward the back of the place. "Bix and Miz Dooley are back there with Tom," the customer said. "The other fellas that was in the shop waiting for the chair took off when she came in. Me, I was already halfway through my shave or I would've took off out of here, too."

Longarm nodded his thanks and went through the doorway into the back room where Tom Bowen's body

lay on a long table. Bowen was naked. The table was surrounded by a rat's nest of bottles and tubes, things Longarm recognized as embalming tools without having any
understanding whatsoever of how they were employed.
Nor did he really want to know. It was one thing to shoot
them but quite another to go through this part of the
process.

Bowen's widow was a careworn little wisp of a woman
with gray hair pulled back in a severe bun. She was wearing a colorless, shapeless dress. Longarm could not decide
if this was her idea of a widow's weeds or if she simply
dressed this way all the time for lack of anything else to
wear to town.

"Ma'am," he said, taking his hat off and holding it in
both hands, "I'm awful sorry for your loss. Is there
anything . . . ?"

"You are the man who killed him, aren't you?"

"Yes, ma'am."

Her face screwed up as if she wanted to cry but did
not have enough moisture in her tissues to squeeze any
water out. "I cannot blame you, sir. You did what you
had to do."

"Yes, ma'am. But that don't make the hurting any th'
less. I mean it, ma'am. Is there anything I can do?"

"No. Thank you, but no."

"You should know, Marshal, that the county won't be
paying for the burial," Dooley said. "I talked to Ed Hochavar this morning. The county supervisors say it isn't their
doing, so they won't pay. Miz Bowen will have to."

Longarm took Bix Dooley by the shirtsleeve and
pulled him aside. "How much d'you charge for a
buryin'?"

"Normally, it is five dollars, but . . ."

"But nothin'. This buryin' will be two fifty. I'll pay it my own self. Do you understand me, mister?"

Dooley looked at Longarm's stern expression for only a moment. Then the man nodded. "Two fifty it is, Marshal."

"Thank you." Longarm returned to the widow and nodded to her. "Like I said, ma'am, I just wanted t' express my condolences. I am truly sorry. Where will you . . . will you try an' stay on where you are?"

"No, I don't think so. I will take my children and go back home to Indiana. We have people there. They will take us in." Her voice broke a little but the woman had her pride. She would do what she had to do.

"Yes, ma'am." Longarm bowed his way backward as far as the door, then spun around and got the hell out of there, the stink of the chemicals closing in around him. The chemicals . . . or something.

The barber chair was empty when he returned to the front of the shop. The customer was gone, the apron sheet lying rumpled in the chair.

Chapter 27

Longarm had a light lunch, then ambled over to the same saloon he had patronized the evening before. Other than the bartender the only man in the place was an out-of-work teamster named Gary McCarthy who liked to play draw poker . . . and was so bad a player that even at low stakes Longarm ended the afternoon more than seven dollars to the good.

He was almost ashamed of himself for taking advantage of McCarthy. Almost, not quite. If the man was going to play he should accept the result and did without complaint.

Eventually, his stomach rumbling in search of a meal, Longarm stood up, stretched, and excused himself. "Time t' go have some supper," he said.

McCarthy nodded and began shuffling the cards again, ready for whoever else came in.

Longarm thought about Angela Morris. He smiled. He could not think of a better thing to do with his winnings than to buy her a supper. Then whatever happened afterward, well, that would be good, too.

He walked over to her store and once inside put the CLOSED sign in the window.

"Angela?" She was not in the small, display area. Must be in the back, he thought.

He started to open the door to the back area where the spare stock—and the rumpled bed—was.

"Don't," Angela's voice came past the crack in the door before he had a chance to get inside. "Don't . . . don't come in."

She sounded odd. There was something in the tone of her voice that he did not like. Fear? He thought perhaps so.

Longarm pushed the door a little further open.

"Please don't come inside," she said, her voice definitely quavering.

"Are you all right?" he called.

"Who is it? Who's out there?" Angela responded.

"It's me. Custis Long. From yesterday."

"Custis, I . . . I'm not decent."

"Oh, I've seen . . ." Before he finished the sentence he finished opening the door and began to step inside.

Angela was there all right. So was her husband, Larry Morris, the same asshole Longarm had the run-in with the previous evening.

The man had Angela's skirt and knickers off. She was wearing only her blouse and shirtwaist. Larry was fully clothed but his fly was unbuttoned and his pecker was out, standing stiff and tall. It was not very big, and under Longarm's gaze it began to shrivel.

It was obvious that Angela had been crying. Her face was tear-streaked and puffy. Her chest was heaving and there were large, ugly bruises forming on her upper thighs. Morris was either in the process of raping the woman or had already done so.

"Get out," the man screamed. "You aren't wanted here."

"Angela?" Longarm asked. "D'you want him here? Maybe we both o' us should go." Longarm smiled, no mirth at all in the expression. "Maybe I should take this son of a bitch in an' lock him up on a charge of, oh, domestic violence, maybe."

Longarm took a step forward into the crowded room and Morris screeched, "Don't. Not a step closer."

The man produced a knife from somewhere and flicked it open. He grabbed Angela by the hair and yanked her backward. He held the edge of the blade to the side of her throat. Longarm could see her pulse throbbing in the big artery in her very tender flesh.

"Not a step closer or the woman dies," Morris threatened.

Longarm slowly and deliberately took his .45 out of its leather and cocked it. "Seems t' me, mister, that you've brought a knife to a gunfight. Reckon my revolver trumps your knife."

"I'm telling you, I'll kill her," Morris snarled.

Longarm turned his head, spat, and appeared to ponder that threat for a moment. Then he nodded. "All right. Then what?"

"What?" Morris sounded incredulous.

"I said if you follow through on that an' murder the lady, then what's your plan? This here .45 will shoot right through a little lady like Angela. It'll shoot right inta you. Or you won't be able t' hold a dead woman up for very long. Besides, with all that blood flowin' she'll get slippery. Hard t' hold up once she's all slick-wet with blood. Damn stuff is awful slippery. Did you know that? Then when she drops I'll have a clean shot at you. I'll aim for the belly.

Take you days t' die, prob'ly. By the time you do you'll be screaming for somebody t' have the kindness of puttin' you out of your pain. But nobody will.

"Or you might could kill her an' then real quick surrender. I'd be duty bound to take you in on a charge o' murder. If that happens I can pretty much guarantee you'll hang. Might take a spell for the law t' get around to it. You'll set in an eight-by-eight cell for could be half a year before they finally take you out to the gallows an' put the noose 'round your neck." He grinned. "Reckon I'd like t' come back up and watch you swing when it happens."

"Jesus, mister, I . . . it ain't supposed to work like that," Morris protested.

"What, there's rules about this sort of thing?" Longarm asked.

"Well, yeah," Morris said. "I mean, the deal is if you don't do what I say, I'll kill Angie here."

Longarm shrugged. "An' the rest o' that deal is, if you do, then I'll put a bullet through your face an' another one in your gut."

"I'll kill her. I swear I will."

"You already said that," Longarm reminded the man. "You said that an' I said what I said an' now it's up to you t' decide how you want this t' play out. You go to jail on a charge of domestic violence an' spend a week in lockup or I shoot you or you hang. But whatever you want t' do it's all up to you, mister."

Morris was sweating now. His knife blade was pressed hard against Angela's throat. It was a wonder she was not already bleeding.

"Make up your mind," Longarm said.

Then Angela made the decision for them. She fainted dead away and dropped out of Larry's grip.

Longarm took aim on the center of the man's forehead and said, "All right. My turn. But it ain't a threat, it's a choice. Either turn around an' put your hands back where I can cuff them, or I shoot you down where you stand."

Larry Morris meekly turned around and tossed his now-useless knife onto the bed.

Chapter 28

Town Marshal John Bennett closed the cell door with a loud clang, turned the key to securely lock Larry Morris on the other side of the bars, and took the key ring with him into the other room. "You'll need to sign a complaint," he told Longarm. Bennett pulled his top desk drawer open and dropped the keys into it.

"If you don't mind, Marshal," Bennett said, "I'll prepare the complaint in the morning. It's getting a little late and my old lady has supper on the stove for me. Would that be all right?"

"Fine," Longarm said. "I can't leave until the next southbound stage comes through, so I reckon I'll still be here in the morning. I'll come by right after breakfast if that works good for you."

Bennett nodded. "Fine. I'll see you then." He started for the door.

Longarm paused, curious. "You don't have a night deputy?"

"No, sir, I don't. No room for it in the town budget."

"What d'you do if you have problems at night?" Longarm asked.

Bennett grinned. "I tend to them in the morning."

"Of course," Longarm said. "Fine, then. Good night, John. I'll see you tomorrow morning."

Longarm returned to Angela's shop. The CLOSED sign was in place, but he tapped on the door until she finally came to see who it was. She was fully dressed now but had changed her blouse in addition to retrieving her skirt.

"Custis. What . . . ?"

"I came t' see are you all right."

"I am. Really."

"If you say so, but I thought you might like a store-bought meal this evenin'. That's what I come by to ask you t' begin with." He grinned. "I got some poker winnin's burning a hole in my pocket, an' I can't think of anyone I'd ruther squander them on than you."

"Custis, that is so nice of you."

"Does that mean you'll dine with me?"

"Yes. Thank you."

"Then you pick where y' want to eat. Pick the nicest place in town," he said.

"There aren't so awfully many to choose from."

"Still," he said, "you pick out the nicest there is. That's where we'll go."

Angela giggled. "The town will be scandalized, me going out with a gentleman who is not my husband."

"I thought you said he's your ex-husband."

"I may have exaggerated a little. Does it matter?"

"Not to me, it don't," Longarm said, offering his arm to her.

"Wait a second. I need to get a shawl."

Angela disappeared into her shop again. Longarm was

left wondering if he would ever meet a woman who could simply walk out with a man without first having to do something—anything—else.

Still, the wait was worth doing. Angela was pleasant company at dinner. And afterward in her bed, too.

Chapter 29

The trip down to Lead was unpleasant. A stagecoach was not the most comfortable mode of transportation to begin with and this trip was made even more so by the presence of a drunk who had puked all over himself shortly before boarding the coach. His stench was nearly unbearable, to the point that Longarm chose to leave the padded bench inside and to ride instead perched atop the luggage that was piled on the roof of the vehicle.

If nothing else it made him damned glad to reach Lead. And Lead, Dakota Territory, was such a drab and ugly destination that it took a powerful discomfort to find Lead as the desirable alternative.

Still, Lead was where at least one of the stolen shipments had been consigned. Longarm climbed down from the roof of the Bastrop stagecoach, groaning and grumbling and thinking the trip might have been easier if he had just thought to throw the stinking passenger out on the road. Let the son of a bitch walk to wherever he was going.

"Here's your bag, mister," the jehu said, disengaging

Longarm's carpetbag from the jumble of bags and boxes and dropping it down to him.

"Thanks, Harry." Longarm saluted the man with a forefinger to the brim of his Stetson. Then he picked up his bag and carried it inside the Bastrop office for safe-keeping until he knew what he would be doing later.

"Where can I find the Golden Star?" he asked the station agent. "I'll be wanting the company office if it's different from the mine."

"The Star has a office in town here. 'Nuther one out at the mine site."

"In town I'd think," Longarm said.

The old fellow who was running things for Bastrop grunted and said, "The town place is over top of the hardware. Next street over and a block down. The stairs you want is on the west side of the building."

Longarm thanked the man, parked his bag beside the door, and left in search of the Golden Star offices. When he got there he found a sign hanging on the doorknob saying the staff had gone to lunch and would be back in half an hour. He had no idea when that sign had been hung. Or if anyone was really watching the clock to get back at any particular time, so he returned to the street and went looking for a lunch of his own.

The steak he ordered was almost too tough to chew, the potatoes were undercooked, and the bread tasted like it was made with more sawdust than flour. But other than that the meal was . . . lousy.

The good thing was that it killed enough time that the Golden Star office was open when he returned.

"Good afternoon, sir," he was greeted when he stepped inside. The speaker was a plump woman who was on the shady side of middle age. She had graying hair pulled up in a bun and a chest that drooped within inches of her waist. Or would have had she had a definable waist. Longarm wasn't sure that she had one.

She smiled when she said hello, though. She had a very nice smile, warm and welcoming. Longarm snatched his hat off and introduced himself.

"How can I help you, Marshal?" she asked.

"I'm here about the stagecoach robberies that've been takin' place lately. Can I speak to the manager, please?"

The lady smiled. "I am Zerelda Hughes, marshal."

He waited but that seemed to be the end of what she was saying. Finally he put in, "Yes, ma'am? The, uh, the manager?"

"Excuse me. I thought you might have been told. I do have an operations manager. He is out at the mine, of course." She smiled. "Managing. I run the office in town here. I also own the Golden Star. Which was also the name of my place in Virginia City, which financed this mine. Now what is it that I can do for you, Marshal?"

"My apologies, Miz Hughes. I didn't mean t' offend."

"Nor have you." She motioned him to a chair and sat behind the desk that dominated the room. She shrugged. "I know little enough, Marshal. We lost two payroll shipments. Two out of many. This mine is four and a half years old. I pay my men every week and deal with a bank in Miles City. They ship my payroll in, in specie, weekly. My guess is that the robbers were not targeting my payroll, although considering their take I would say these people had advance knowledge of the much larger shipments of cash to the Deadwood banks. My losses were no more than a pimple on the butts of those bank transfers."

"Did you have insurance?" Longarm asked.

The plainspoken woman nodded. "Or to be more accurate, Marshal, the carrier had their shipments insured."

"And it paid off?"

Again she nodded. "To the penny. My people's pay was delayed but they received their full pay, just a week late." She smiled. "You would think their throats had been cut but the next week they made up for it with their carousing. The saloons made out all right. They ran tabs for my workers and were also paid a week late. The only ones who really suffered were the whores. If I had been running a whorehouse in town I would have run a tab for the boys there, too, but the idiots who own those didn't have business sense enough to think of that."

Longarm grinned. "I'll bet you would have made a fortune if you ran a whorehouse."

Zerelda Hughes threw her head back and laughed. Then she said, "Marshal, I did in fact make a fortune running a whorehouse in Virginia City. A very fine whorehouse if I do say so myself."

"Do you know much about the robberies?" Longarm asked. "Other than the obvious, I mean. D'you know anything you think might help me catch up with the SOBs that robbed you?"

She shook her head. "Only what I've already mentioned. I think they were after those bank transfers and got my little payroll as a sort of bonus. They certainly don't try to steal every shipment, and I have a payroll come in every week without fail. But what sticks in my mind is that every time they do hit there is some serious money involved. I think they know in advance that the prize will be worth taking."

"I agree with you, Miz Hughes. How much is your payroll anyway?"

"Two hundred eighty dollars, Marshal. Delivered every Friday, paid every Saturday. Small potatoes compared with what those Deadwood banks lost."

"Did your local law investigate the robberies?"

"No. There was no jurisdiction, of course. Anyway, poor Tommy would have been out of his depth with something serious like that. He can keep the Saturday-night drunks from tearing up the saloons and the whorehouses, but that is about the extent of his usefulness. Truly, I think if you want to get to the bottom of these robberies, you need to look in Deadwood. Perhaps in the bank there?" She shrugged. "It is just a suggestion, of course. I wish I could do something to genuinely help, but I know very little. And was hurt by those robberies not at all. I have no dog in this hunt."

Longarm smiled. "I kinda wish I had known you when you was a young'un, Miz Hughes."

"I shall take that as a compliment, Marshal."

"Good," he said, "because that is how 'twas meant." He stood and put the Stetson back on. "Thanks for your help, ma'am, an' good luck to you."

Chapter 30

"Poor Tommy" was indeed as useless as Zerelda Hughes said he was. The man was huge, standing half a head taller than Longarm and Longarm was no dwarf. His beef was no doubt the reason he had the job; he was big enough to break up a brawl without having to call for help, and the mere size of him would be enough to intimidate all but the craziest drunk.

That said, if the man had a brain in his head Longarm could find no evidence of it.

"I don' know shit 'bout it," was the town marshal's comment when Longarm asked about the robberies.

Two minutes of Tommy Rabineaux was more than enough for Longarm. He quickly thanked the man and went back to the Bastrop office.

"I suppose you want to ask about the holdups," the elderly company agent, Charles Stude, said.

"Yes, sir," Longarm told him. "Anything you know, anything you care to guess."

"What I know you could fit onto the head of a hatpin," Stude said. "What I can guess is even less. I've been wracking my brains about this and can't come up with a damn thing except to think that those fellows knew what to expect when they robbed our stages though more about the Deadwood end of it than ours. I think our losses could be considered almost an accident."

That was the same thing Longarm assumed and probably for the same reasons.

"Did your insurance company know anything in advance?" he asked.

Stude shrugged and said, "Not that I know of, but for that you would really have to talk with our agent where the shipments originated. That would be up in Miles City."

"All right, thanks. When will the next coach run to Deadwood?"

"We don't have anything now until tomorrow, but Fremont has a coach going over there this evening." He grinned and added, "I probably wouldn't mention that if you were a paying passenger. It wouldn't be right to take a fare away from the company. Should be okay, though, since you federal fellas ride free."

Longarm thanked the man and retrieved his bag. He would have to find the Fremont Stage Company office and arrange a seat on their coach over to Deadwood—it was only a few miles from Lead—then see what he could find in the way of dinner.

Chapter 31

The last time Longarm was in Deadwood there was at least a little green foliage visible on the hillsides and up the creek bank. Now all of that was gone, probably harvested for firewood. Now the town was little but mud and smoke and the chemical stink of the acids used in the process of extracting gold from crushed rock.

It was not a pretty town. It was, however, a vibrant, lively, exhilarating town and Longarm liked it. He thanked the jehu on the Fremont coach, collected his bag—at least on the short drive over from Lead he had not had to share the coach with a smelly drunk—and headed for Georgia Whitcomb's boardinghouse.

He had stayed with Georgia twice in the past and enjoyed her company.

She also happened to be a genuinely good fuck.

"Custis!" she yelped with a smile and a kiss when she saw him. "You should have wired ahead. I could have prepared something special for you."

"Georgia dear, you *are* something special," he shot

back at her, wrapping the woman in his arms and lifting
her off the floor with his hug.

Georgia was probably in her forties but looked years
younger. She was a petite blonde with tits twice as large
as a woman her size had any right to.

He set her feet back down onto the porch outside her
boardinghouse and began to give her a proper kiss, but
when he tried to slide his tongue past her lips she turned
her head away.

"Georgia, what . . . ?"

"No, Custis, I can't."

"D'you take a vow of chastity or somethin'?" he
asked.

"No, I . . . I'm married."

"You are. Well, I think that man is one lucky fella. Do
I know him? When'd this happen? What kinda man is he?"

She laughed and pulled away from his embrace. "So
many questions," she said, linking her arm into his and
leading him inside the house. "His name is Ben Andrews.
He is superintendent of the Agnes Mine here. He is even
more handsome than you are, Custis, and I love him to
pieces."

"Then I say again, Georgia, he is one very fortunate
fella, because you are worth more than any gold he could
pull outta the ground." He smiled and gave Georgia a
chaste kiss on the forehead.

"Ben should be home at six thirty. I can't wait for you
to meet him. You will stay with me, won't you? In spite
of not being able to . . . you know."

"Yes, dear, I'll want t' stay here in spite of not bein'
able to . . . you know." He gave her another very brief
hug and asked, "My same room available?"

"Yes, of course. The truth is that I'm not taking board-
ers any longer. Ben makes a good living for us, and he

didn't like the idea of having strangers in the house. He asked me to quit."

"Well, in that case I can go over to the hotel an' get a room," Longarm said.

"You will do no such thing, Custis. You are welcome to stay but as a friend and not a customer."

"You're a doll, Georgia, but you know the government can afford to pay you something for putting me up."

"No, sir, I won't hear of it. You are our guest. Just like before, you come and go however you please. Can you tell me what business you are here about this time? Come into the parlor and sit. I'll get us some tea and scones, and you can tell me all about it. Or at least the part you're allowed to speak of."

"Oh, I reckon I'm allowed t' talk about it. It's no secret."

"Good. Then sit right down here . . . not that chair, please, it's Ben's favorite spot . . . and wait while I get the tea and scones. Then we can talk. You can tell me about your criminals, and I can tell you all about how I met Ben."

Chapter 32

Longarm stepped into Graziano's Saloon with a sigh of relief. "Rye whiskey an' a chaser," he told the barkeep, laying a quarter down on the bar.

"You look beat, mister," the barman ventured.

"I feel like I been run over, stomped on, an' wore out. Ah, thanks." He downed the shot and took a gulp of the beer. "Let's do that again."

The bartender poured another belt of rye and Longarm tossed that one back as quickly as the first, adding to the quarter that remained on the bar.

He did indeed feel worn out after dining with the lovebirds. Georgia's cooking was every bit as good as he remembered, but a fine meal was a helluva price to pay for having to eat with the two of them.

The thing was, the new husband, Ben, was a talker. Not just an ordinary talker, either. This man was a marathon talker. And boring. His mouth never closed, not even when he was chewing his food. Little flakes of this dish or that spattered off his lips throughout the meal. Watching him was enough to make Longarm sick. Looking elsewhere helped, but there was no escaping the voice.

The man droned. About anything. About everything. Longarm's head hurt from listening to him.

"Another?" the barman asked.

"No, not yet," Longarm said. He left the empty shot glass where it was but picked up his beer and carried it with him to a table where a foursome were engaged in some stud poker.

"Care to sit in with us, mister?" one of the gents offered. "Low stakes. Nothing serious."

"I would, thanks," Longarm said. "Long as you boys don't try an' talk my ears off."

One of the fellows raised an eyebrow at that but the men made no comment and asked no questions. They merely nodded to an empty chair.

Longarm pulled some money out of his pockets and settled in for the evening.

If he played his cards right—literally and figuratively, too—he could sit here at the poker table until Ben quit talking and went up to bed.

Longarm snickered as a thought struck him. He would have to ask Georgia about it come morning. The question was, did Ben talk in his sleep, too?

Likely, Longarm thought.

He also wondered how long politeness would require him to remain a guest in the house. As soon as it was reasonably possible, he thought, he would move his things over to a hotel and get away from Ben Andrews.

Chapter 33

Town Marshal Noogie DiNunzio—Longarm had no idea what the man's real first name was—was a close acquaintance if not quite a close friend. After all the man was a teetotaler and who could have a true friend with such radical leanings. On the other hand, he did have other vices.

Still, he was happy to see the man. Noogie was snoring behind his desk when Longarm came into his office the following morning. With a wide grin showing beneath his mustache, Longarm tiptoed across the slate floor and came down hard with both hands flat on the desktop, at the same time letting out a screech that would have made a Comanche proud.

Noogie nearly came out of his skin.

"Long! You son of a bitch."

Longarm laughed. "Nice t' see you, too, Noogie."

"Damn you, I think I shit my pants."

Longarm loudly sniffed, then with a solemn nod said, "Yeah, hoss, it kinda smells like you did."

DiNunzio came out of his chair and gave Longarm a bearhug, not necessarily easy for a man a head shorter and thirty pounds lighter than Longarm. "It's good to see you, y' old son of a bitch."

"Good t' see you, too, Noogie."

"What brings you up here to God's country?"

"The recent stagecoach holdups, Noogie."

DiNunzio looked puzzled. "Those aren't federal jurisdiction."

Longarm grinned. "They are now." He explained about Cheyenne mail clerk Clarence Osgood and his little ruse.

DiNunzio slapped his thigh and chuckled. "I like that, I do."

"It gives us a peg to hang some serious time on. If we can catch the assholes that are doing it, anyhow. Do you know anything, Noogie? Hear any rumors? Anything at all?"

"You know I wish I could help you, hoss, but I haven't heard a thing. I'll take you around and introduce you to the bankers, of course. I know they'll be pleased to know that you're on the case for whatever that's worth. Then tonight you are gonna be my guest for supper. There's a place in town . . . I'm pretty sure it's new since the last time you were here . . . they have the best meat you ever put a tooth to, I guar-own-tee it."

Longarm feigned shock. He put a hand to his chest and flapped it like he was feeling his beating heart.

"What, you don't think we can come up with some decent food in this town?" Noogie asked, acting insulted.

"No, you idiot, I didn't think you knew how t' pay for a meal. I thought all you local coppers walked around with your hands in other people's pockets."

"Aw, Longarm, you know that's politicians you're thinking of."

Longarm slapped himself on the forehead. "Silly me. Of course."

"So how's about you buy us some coffee. We can sit and tell some lies and you can fill me in on everywhere you've been and everything you've done since the last time I saw you."

"Sounds fine t' me, Noogie. Lead the way."

Chapter 34

Chatting over coffee was pleasant enough, but it did not get the job done. After no more than three cups of coffee and a piled-high plate of crullers, it was time to get down to work.

Noogie took Longarm first to the Charter Bank of Deadwood, where the manager practically wept to know there was a federal man on the case.

"You can't know how important this is to us, Marshal," the banker said.

"Didn't you have insurance?" Longarm asked.

"Oh, we did indeed. After the first two holdups the stagecoach line refused to insure our money shipments. After the next two our insurance carrier raised our rates and said they would drop us as customers if another shipment was stolen."

"No wonder you're anxious to get this problem resolved," Longarm said.

"Anything I can do, Marshal. Really. Anything at all. You just let me know, and it's yours."

"Information is what I need now," Longarm told the man. "Anything you know and everything you guess."

The banker merely shrugged. "I wish I did know."

They walked over to the Fremont Stage Company office and spoke with the manager there with no greater result. He knew nothing helpful but offered any assistance Longarm might require.

At the next stop, Noogie introduced Longarm to a tall, balding fellow named Tom Bligh. He was every bit as eager to help.

Longarm asked the routine questions including, "Who in the bank knew to expect a transfer of cash?"

"I'm the only one who knows in advance," Bligh said, "and I don't mention it to my people." He sighed and said, "For probably the same reasons that you are asking the question. I can tell you with certainty that none of my people got wind of the shipments and tipped off the robbers."

Bligh grimaced. "Just last week there was another robbery. Same deal all the way around. Two people in dusters with flour-sack hoods and what I am told were very large shotguns. They took everything."

Longarm grunted.

"It's like I told you," Noogie said. "None of us can figure it out, Longarm. I truly hope you can come up with something."

"So do I," Longarm admitted. "So do I."

Chapter 35

"We might see Tom again later," Noogie said as they left the bank.

Longarm raised an eyebrow, but DiNunzio did not add to the comment. Instead he changed the subject and pointed down the street toward a tall building that was obviously a commercial establishment of some sort but had no sign posted outside.

"That's our other bank," he said, "but there's no point in us talking to them."

"They haven't been robbed?" Longarm asked.

"Nope. But then they're a different sort of bank. I don't understand it, really, but they're what they call an invest-ment bank. They deal mostly in paper and promises, not cash. They're for the high rollers, not for us working guys." Noogie smiled. "Anyway, I got some things I need to do. What do you say I meet you back at my office about, oh, six o'clock. We'll go have supper and then I'll take you to a place that I like." He winked. "You'll like it, too, and that's a promise."

"What sort of . . .?"

DiNunzio held his hand up to stop the questioning. "You'll see. Trust me."

Longarm grinned. "The last time you told me that I damn near got shot by a jealous husband."

"Hey, give me a break here. How was I to know the woman was married!"

"All right. I'll trust you. But just this one more time." Longarm laughed. "I'll see you about six then, Noogie."

Longarm left his friend and collected his carpetbag from Georgia, making the excuse that he needed to be able to observe the activities in town. Part of the job he was on, he explained. He did not mention the new husband's incessant commentary as the reason for his flight from Georgia's house. Instead he gave her a kiss on the cheek and his thanks and let it go at that.

He carried his bag in town and stopped at the first hotel he came to. The place was not grand, but it appeared to be clean . . . and there was no Ben Andrews present to talk his ears off.

"Of course we'll take your voucher for payment. You're a deputy marshal, you say? Wonderful. That should make us safer, just having you here, right? Your room is upstairs and to the left. Number six. I hope you enjoy your stay with us." The clerk handed Longarm a key with a numbered tag dangling from it and pointed to the staircase.

"Send up some hot water, please."

"Do you need a tub or just a pitcher?"

"A pitcher will do," Longarm told the man, rubbing his cheek to check the state of his whiskers. He definitely needed a wash and a shave before whatever Noogie had in mind because whatever it was, it was apt to involve women. The ladies were Noogie's vice, as Longarm learned long since.

Not that he was complaining, he thought with a wry smile as he stripped off his clothes and dipped a cloth into the basin of warm water.

Chapter 36

"You're right," Longarm said as they walked out of the restaurant, picking his teeth and rubbing his very full belly. "That was the best meal I've had in a long while."

"Glad you enjoyed it." DiNunzio smiled. "Now we get to the good part of the evening."

"And that would be . . . ?"

DiNunzio's smile only got wider. He did not explain.

He led Longarm to a quiet—or at least as quiet as Deadwood seemed to get—residential street at the edge of town and to a two-story house with flowerpots on the porch and lamps glowing in the windows.

"You'll like this place," Noogie said as they mounted the steps and approached the front door.

Longarm looked but there were no obvious indications of just exactly what sort of place it was. He could, however, guess.

Noogie tapped lightly on the door, which was promptly opened by a huge man, black as night and so filled with health and vitality that he looked like he had been oiled.

His smile when he saw DiNunzio was wide. "Marshal. Welcome. Come inside, sir."

Noogie beamed as he turned toward Longarm and said, "Dennis, this is my old friend Custis Long. Custis, this is Dennis Demaio." He laughed. "With a name like that we think Dennis must be Italian. Me and him could even be related."

"Don't pay attention to him, Marshal," the bouncer said. "We don't pay him any mind."

Demaio had a slight accent. British, Longarm thought? He wanted to ask where the man was from but refrained, common courtesy overcoming curiosity.

"Come inside. Please," Demaio said, ushering them into an opulently furnished parlor. "Miss Theresa will be out in a moment. Please sit down. She will be out in a moment."

There were several whores already in the room. Two of them squealed with joy when they saw DiNunzio enter. The girls were young and pretty and elegantly dressed.

Miss Theresa, Longarm thought, must surely deal with an upper-crust clientele. He wondered how Noogie could afford girls like these on a town marshal's salary.

Longarm was halfway across the room when it occurred to him that Dennis had greeted him as "Marshal." He was only introduced by name, not by title.

Before he had time to chew on that thought the room was suddenly filled to overflowing with the presence of Miss Theresa.

Theresa Bullea was slim, elegant, every inch what Longarm thought of as a lady. When she spoke her accent matched Dennis's. Probably, he guessed, the two came from the same distant place. They must have been together for some length of time.

"What a pleasure to meet you, Marshal Long," she said, extending her hand.

On an impulse, instead of shaking the woman's hand, Longarm bowed over it and kissed the air a half inch or so above the woman's warm, scented flesh.

Theresa had light brown hair done up and pinned. She had golden brown eyes and a heart-shaped mouth. She was fairly tall for a woman, probably five feet six or seven. Her perfume was delicate, the scent indefinable. Not flowery but very sensual. But then Theresa herself was very sensual. An aura of sexuality surrounded her.

Longarm felt himself growing hard just from being in the same room with her. "My pleasure, ma'am," he said.

"Please. Sit. Make this your home while you visit us here in our dear little Deadwood." She made a moue. "Such a terrible name for such a dear town, no?"

Longarm found himself agreeing with her. Hell, he would have agreed with this woman if she said the sun was blue. And never mind that Deadwood, Dakota Territory, was a noisy, stinking, muddy hellhole of a place. If Theresa Bullea said it was a dear little place, well, then it was one awfully damn dear little place. End of subject.

"Custis is your name, yes?" she said, taking his arm and guiding him to a comfortable chair. "I had an uncle named Custis. Such a nice name. But oh, such a terrible end for my dear uncle. He died, you see. In Africa. Killed by some Hottentot or"—she waved her hand dismissively—"or one of those aborigines. I can't begin to keep them straight." She laughed—delightfully, Longarm thought—and added, "Even Dennis cannot keep them straight, and he comes from one of them."

Theresa motioned to one of the girls, a stunning redhead with porcelain skin and artificially red lips, and said, "Bring the marshal anything he likes, Agnes." She turned back to Longarm, cocked her head to the side in thought, and said, "Let me see, your preference is for rye whiskey, is it not? Rye, Agnes. Our best."

Noogie had been following them. He said, "The usual for me, Aggie. Theresa, these robberies are sure to be cleared up now that Longarm is here. He's the best there is."

"Is that why he is here, Noogie? Oh, I am so glad." She shuddered. "We all worry." To Longarm she said, "We are accustomed to the occasional strong-arm robbery. Even to a holdup now and then. But these road agents are frightening. I am afraid to have a drive in my phaeton." She shook her head sadly. "And transporting my girls here from the east. It is all quite discouraging."

"Don't worry, Theresa," Noogie said. "My pal Longarm already has some ideas about this. Those highwaymen will be behind bars before you can say Yankee Doodle."

That was news to Longarm, but then Noogie never had been one to worry about anything as inconsequential as the truth when there were women involved.

Agnes returned with a tall drink for Longarm and a cup of steaming coffee for Noogie the teetotaler. A second girl, just as beautiful but a head shorter, was with her carrying a tray of iced cookies.

Longarm was still full from dinner, but . . . the cookies were every bit as good as they looked.

And the girls were not so bad-looking, either.

Noogie DiNunzio's idea of a pleasant evening was not entirely terrible, Longarm decided.

Chapter 37

"Agnes, we will not be needing your services, thank you."

"But, Miss Terry . . ."

"Tish tosh, dear. No 'buts' if you please. I shall see that you are properly compensated." She linked her arm into Longarm's. "Tonight the marshal is mine, dear."

"Yes, miss." The girl bobbed her head and turned away.

It occurred to Longarm that "Miss Terry" ran a tight ship here. There would be no backtalk or misbehavior from her girls.

And what a splendid cadre of girls they were. While Longarm sipped his drink—the rye really was superb; he wondered where the hell she found it because he would love to lay in a supply of his own when he got back to Denver—a bevy of beauties wandered in and out of the parlor, as did a small but steady flow of customers, all of whom seemed to belong in the upper end of Deadwood's social register.

There were girls of all description. Tall and short,

blond and brunette. White, black, brown, and yellow. And every one a beauty. There was even a fat girl with one leg. Longarm had no idea what sort of man might want her but obviously there was a need for her services or she would not be here.

Terry rested her hand on Longarm's leg. On his thigh, actually. Very high up on his thigh.

She looked down and could hardly miss seeing the lump in his trousers caused by his hard-on, which had only become more insistent now that she was seated practically in his lap.

Terry laughed and leaned close to whisper, "Interested?" He was aware of the warmth of her breath in his ear almost as much as the meaning of that single word.

By way of an answer he reached over to cup her left breast in his hand and gently squeeze.

Terry laughed, took that hand in hers and stood. "Ladies," she announced, "if there is anything short of the house catching fire, take your difficulties to Dennis. I shall be busy, thank you."

Head high and smiling, she led Longarm through a narrow hallway into the back of the house where she had a suite of private rooms, including her office.

And a bedroom.

Quite a bedroom, in fact.

It was beautifully furnished in mahogany and satin, the predominant colors pink and white. The lady definitely had a fine and discriminating taste.

"Do you like?" she asked.

"Oh, yes," he said, looking not at the room but into Theresa's eyes.

"Good," she responded. "Would you like a drink?"

He had no recollection of what he might have done with the first drink he was given, but it was no longer in his hand. "No," he said. "Everything I'm interested in is right here." He maintained eye contact with her throughout the comment.

Theresa's smile became wider. "Then why delay?" she asked.

Theresa stepped gracefully over to the side of the bed and began removing her gown.

Chapter 38

"I wish I was an artist," Longarm said.

Terry's eyebrows rose and she said, "What a very odd comment."

"No, I mean it. I'd like t' be able to paint you, just exactly the way you look right now."

Her smile became kittenish. She struck a pose, one leg placed slightly ahead of the other. Head high and back arched to better show off her tits, which were firm, high, and pink-tipped.

"I'll be damned," he blurted when she turned to face him squarely. His eyes were drawn to her crotch where there was . . . nothing. No hair. Not a strand.

He laughed. "I'd like t' know who your barber is so's I can go watch you getting that shave."

"Then perhaps I shall allow you to watch the next time Dennis shaves me." She lifted her arms to show that she had no underarm hair, either. In fact he could not find a bit of hair anywhere other than on her head. "Do you like it?" she asked.

He hesitated while he pondered that question. Then he nodded. "Yeah. I think I do."

"It is especially nice when one is performing cunnilingus," Terry said.

"Cunning-what?"

"Eating pussy, silly."

"Ah. That I do understand."

"Have you ever eaten a bald pussy?"

"No, I reckon not."

"Then you must try it, my dear."

"Yeah," he said, "I really oughta do that."

"I can't think of any better time than the present."

"D'you think so?"

"Oh, indeed I do." She stepped close to him and quickly unbuttoned him, yanking his clothing off in a mad hurry now.

When they both were naked Longarm bent, scooped her behind the knees, and carried her to the big bed. He deposited the woman there and lay down beside her.

Terry's mouth was fresh. She tasted lightly of mint. Her tongue was hot and eager, probing his mouth at the same time as he was investigating hers. Her breath began to quicken. He took that as his cue to take things a step further.

He reached for her right breast. Cupped it. Squeezed it. Rolled her nipple, now very hard, between his thumb and forefinger.

"Lick me," she demanded.

This, he was reminded, was a woman who was accustomed to giving orders and to being obeyed. Custis Long was no woman's pet dog on a leash. But in this case he did not mind obeying Theresa Bullea. He bent his head to her left tit and licked and suckled that nipple, then shifted to the other.

"Now my pussy, dear. Lick me."

Longarm grunted. And wriggled down across her belly to her naked cunt, his tongue moving across her flesh as he went.

Terry was right. It was . . . different . . . eating a pussy that had no hair. She tasted fresh and clean down there, too. She must just have finished douching before she joined them in the parlor.

He fleetingly wondered if that timing was coincidence. Or if she had had this in mind even before she met him.

No, probably not, he realized. She knew there was a deputy U.S. marshal in town, that much was obvious, but she could not have known what he looked like or that she would be attracted to him.

As for whether he would be attracted to her, hell, he could not think of a man alive who would not be.

Terry began to moan and to writhe beneath his fluttering tongue, and Longarm went back to paying attention to business. He did not want to waste a moment's awareness while he was with this exceptionally beautiful woman.

Chapter 39

"Nice," he murmured. Longarm was lying on Terry's bed, propped up with four feather pillows and with an ashtray resting on his chest.

"Better than merely nice," she said as she trimmed the twist off a cigar and popped it into his mouth. She struck a match and lighted the panatela for him, then stretched out beside him. "If I could find more men like you, dear man, I could open a bordello for ladies. You are that good."

"If you could find more that're really like me, darlin', you couldn't get them t' work in your whorehouse. They'd be wanting more t' life than just the night."

She sighed. "I suppose you are right about that. Men do tend to like to work." Terry chuckled. "As it happens, I like my work rather well, too." She reached over and plucked the cigar out of his mouth, held it to her own rouged lips and took a drag and then returned it to him.

"Thinking of work," she said, "tell me about yours."

Longarm shrugged. "Damn, this cigar is mild," he said.

"Oh, go ahead. Tell me about your search for those robbers. Noogie said you have some leads. What are they?"

"Nothing, really. Noogie tends t' exaggerate things, y'know."

"Well if you don't *want* to tell me," she pouted.

"No, I'm serious. There's nothing t' tell. Yet."

"But soon. Do you think you will know something soon?"

He shrugged again. "You never know 'bout these things. The only thing I can tell you for sure is that I'll keep after 'em."

"Until they are dead?"

"My purpose ain't to kill, darlin'. I'd ruther bring 'em in for trial."

"And hanging?"

"In this country we don't hang folks for robbing. For murder we do, but not for robbing."

"Being locked away in jail would be like being killed though, wouldn't it," Terry said.

"To some types of men I suppose it would be. That's their choice, though. They do a crime; they go to prison. It's simple."

"It is barbaric," she said. "But in my country someone can be hanged for robbery."

"Where's that?" he asked.

Terry did not answer. Instead she bounded off the bed and grabbed a dressing gown out of her chifforobe. "Come. Join me. I need to check on my girls and you would like a drink, no?"

"I would like a drink, yes," he said, rising and starting to dress.

He took another long look at Terry before she covered up all that beauty. Damn, but she was a good-looking woman. She had a body as sleek as a seal, and she knew how to use it to please a man.

"Come now," she said when he was dressed. She held her hand out to him, smiling. "We will join whoever is in the parlor, and we shall have a drink together, you and me."

Longarm took her hand and let the tall beauty lead him back into the world.

Chapter 40

Longarm was pleased but not particularly surprised to see E. Thomas Bligh in the parlor. The tall, very nearly bald banker had a drink in one hand and a diminutive Chinese girl in the other.

"Marshal Long," he said enthusiastically when Longarm entered the room. Bligh waved his drink and said, "Join me."

"Do," Terry whispered from behind. "I have work to do."

Longarm turned his head. "Any idea where Noogie might be?"

She laughed. "I know exactly where Marshal DiNunzio is right now. He won't be out for a little longer."

That sounded like Noogie, all right. Longarm accepted another of those excellent rye whiskies from a raven-haired girl and sat in an overstuffed armchair to Bligh's right. The same girl fetched an ottoman for him, even lifted his feet and placed them on the ottoman. Now this, he thought, was service. Finally she settled down on the floor by his legs, one hand on his calf. "If there is anything more . . ." she said.

"I'll let you know." He found it hard to believe when he was just leaving Terry's bed, but this black-haired girl aroused him. She had tits like pillows and an impossibly small waist. He suspected she was one of those southern girls who had surgery to remove their lower ribs so their waists could be smaller. That, of course, made it difficult for them to breathe at times and led to fainting. Or worse. It was damned good to look at, though.

"About those robberies," Bligh said. "How will you go about catching them?"

"Damned if I know," Longarm said, taking a swallow of the rye. The whiskey warmed his belly through and through. "I have no ideas at all right now."

The truth was that he did have an idea or two, but he was loathe to discuss them in public. Not exactly public, of course, but the whores had big ears. There was no telling what they might overhear. And then tell. Or to whom.

Bligh might be comfortable discussing such things where others could hear, but Longarm was not.

"Can I get you anything?" the dark-haired girl asked, rubbing his leg and smiling. She battered her eyelashes. "And I do mean *any*thing."

"Oh, I'd like that just fine," Longarm said, stroking her hair. "But not right now."

"A snack then? Peanuts or popcorn?"

"A bowl o' peanuts would be nice," he said. He didn't so much want the peanuts as he wanted to give the girl something to do.

She leaped up and hustled off, presumably to the kitchen, to get his peanuts.

Longarm leaned back in the very comfortable armchair and helped himself to another swallow of the rye. A man could get used to living in such comfort, he thought.

Chapter 41

Noogie DiNunzio had not yet returned from his romp when Longarm decided to head back to his hotel room for some overdue sleep. He collected his key from the desk clerk and gave the man a friendly "good night," then went up to his room.

Once there he poured a little cold water into the basin, dipped a washcloth in, and wiped himself off before crawling into the lumpy—but very welcome—bed. He felt good—hell, better than good—after his evening with Theresa Bullea. He was thinking of her when he dropped off to sleep.

In the morning he dressed quickly and went downstairs. "Where can I find a good breakfast?" he asked of the person, different from the night clerk, who was on duty behind the desk.

Armed with a little local knowledge, Longarm found a tiny café that catered to the common man. He sat at the counter and surrounded enough eggs, ham, and hotcakes to feed two lumberjacks and their bulldog.

"That," he told the grease-stained fellow behind the

counter, "was about the best meal I've had in a while." It was the truth.

He returned to the street and walked over to the town marshal's office. Noogie was already behind his desk, looking as bright and chipper as always.

"Where'd you go last night?" Noogie asked. "I was just getting started, but they told me you'd already left. Didn't you have a good time?"

"Had 'bout as good a time as a man could have without he keeled over from a heart attack an' died dead away." Longarm winked and said, "I didn't see a cull in that whole herd."

"Terry keeps only the best for herself. Any that don't work out for her she sends over to the casino. Some of the girls work their trade on the floor there. A few, the ones with really good hands, become dealers or croupiers."

"Her casino?" Longarm asked.

Noogie nodded. "Hers and a friend of hers. Say, why don't I take you there tonight? The girls are almost as hot and the tables are dead square. They're the most honest outfit I ever did see. I'm thinking you'll like the place."

"Tonight then," Longarm said.

"Have you had breakfast yet?"

"Just came from there. Now I'm thinking to hunt up a barber and get a shave." He fingered his chin and grinned. "I wouldn't want t' scratch up those sweet young things too bad tonight."

"I tell you what then," Noogie said. "I'll go get my breakfast and meet you at the Bastrop office. I haven't looked into the robberies too close because they've always occurred outside my jurisdiction, but I know the lay of the land so if you don't mind, I'll go with you. We'll interview everyone involved. If I remember correct, the Bastrop driver who was on this end of the run the last time they were hit, he should be pulling in some time this afternoon."

"Do you always keep such close tabs on your town, Noogie?"

"I try to. After all, that's what they pay me for."

"Thinking of which, how the hell can you afford t' do business with Terry's girls? And who paid for my fun last night?"

Noogie waved the question away. "The town don't pay much in the way of salary, but free pussy is one of the benefits. Terry never charges me. Didn't charge for you last night, neither."

Longarm nodded. He had heard of such arrangements in other towns. That sort of perquisite was strictly under the table—or behind the closed door—but it was not unheard of. He was not sure of the ethics involved there, but what was done was done. It could not be taken back.

And considering how good a lay Terry Bullea was he would not want to take it back anyway.

"I'll meet you back here at"—he took his Ingersoll out and looked at the time—"at ten o'clock, say." Since he happened to have the watch out anyway he went ahead and wound the spring, something that had to be done every day.

"Sounds fine," Noogie agreed, getting up and reaching for his hat.

Chapter 42

"To tell you the truth, Marshal, there's not all that much truth to tell," Bastrop jehu Clovis Sensabaugh told them when his coach pulled into Deadwood and a helper was leading the team away. "Do you mind coming with me for a few minutes?"

Longarm raised an eyebrow, but Noogie seemed to know what was going on. "That's fine, Clo," DiNunzio said. "You go ahead. We'll be right behind you."

Longarm took his cue from Noogie and tagged along with the driver to No. 10, the same saloon where James Butler Hickok had been murdered. "A double, Jimmy, and a chaser," Sensabaugh ordered, slapping a half dollar onto the bar.

The jehu downed his whiskey in one gulp and followed it with half of the beer. The bartender immediately filled the whiskey glass again and Sensabaugh tossed that one back, too.

"It's dry work out there," the driver said by way of explanation, "and damned frightening what with those robberies. I don't mind telling you, they scare me plenty.

You never know when the bastards might cut loose with one of those double barrels. You ever see what a shotgun up close can do to a man? I have, and I don't want to see it again. More than that, I don't want to be on the receiving end of one of those blasts. They can damn near cut a man in two." He shuddered and picked up the whiskey glass. Finding it empty he called, "Again, Jimmy. One more time."

While he was waiting for the whiskey to be reloaded he downed the rest of his beer.

"Something to help my nerves," he said. "It always worries me when I pass that spot."

"That spot," Longarm repeated. "D'you mean you were held up at the same spot both times?"

"Yes, sir. Within a couple hundred feet of the same place anyway," Sensabaugh said.

"I wonder," Longarm mused, "if the Fremont coaches were robbed at the same place each time they were hit." He turned to Noogie and asked, "How many times were they robbed?"

"Fremont? Four times. I don't know if all four took place at the same spot or if they were robbed where the Bastrop runs were, but I know how we can find out. Clo here was the Bastrop driver. John Halley was driving for Fremont two of those times that I can recall. Who else was on top for Fremont when they were robbed, Clo?"

The man motioned for his beer mug to be refilled. Apparently he had all the whiskey his nerves needed so he would switch to just the beer now. While Jimmy was drawing another beer, and Sensabaugh was digging in his pocket for another coin, Sensabaugh said, "One time that would be Stanley Applegate. The other time, um, let me think. That was the first holdup. The driver would have been John Dyal. But he's gone now. Said it got too cold up here. He headed back down Arizona way. Or so he said. It might could have been the sight of those twin shotgun barrels. I have nightmares about them, too, so I wouldn't blame the man if that was why he drew his time and moved on."

"Are either Halley or Applegate in town now?" Longarm asked.

"I'm pretty sure Halley is," Noogie said.

"Let's go find out. If he is, I'd like to hire a buggy and all of us drive out along the road to the places where you fellows were held up. It's too late to do that today, but we could start out first thing tomorrow morning."

"What good would that do, Marshal?" Sensabaugh asked.

"I'm not sure it would do any good, Clo, but it's worth a try just on the off chance that we could learn something. Besides," he said with a wink, "if the robbers are in town here an' see what we're doing, it might make them nervous. An' nervous criminals are apt t' fuck up. Can we do that, Noogie?"

"I'm game. You know that."

"Clo?"

"I'm with you, Marshal. There isn't a man anywhere that wants these sons of bitches caught any worse than I do."

Longarm nodded. "Seven o'clock tomorrow morning then? At the livery. We'll hire a rig and go see what we can see."

"Done," Noogie said.

"It's good with me. Tomorrow is my layover day anyhow." Sensabaugh laughed. "There's nothing I'd rather do on my off day than crawl into an outfit and take a drive."

Longarm laid a coin on the bar and said to Jimmy, "Give my friend here another shot and a beer. Noogie, you said something about us having a night on the town so I tell you what, I'll go back to the hotel an' wash up a bit. Then I think it's my turn to buy us a supper. I'll meet you at your office and we can go make an evening of it. An' Clovis, I'll see you tomorrow morning."

"Yes, sir. I'm happy to cooperate any way that I can. I think Halley will be, too."

"If he doesn't want to help," Noogie said, "Fremont will make him want to. They want these robberies to stop."

"I'll stop by the Fremont office an' tell them what we want," Longarm said. He nodded to Sensabaugh and Noogie and left No. 10 and its bloody memories of Hickok.

Chapter 43

Longarm took Noogie to a good-quality café for their supper. The place was neither as fancy nor as expensive as the restaurant where they had eaten the night before, but the food was good and the price was right. When they finished their meal Longarm retrieved his Stetson from the rack beside the front door and said, "All right. Where's this casino you were talking about earlier?"

"It's close enough we can walk to it," DiNunzio said.

"Lead the way then. I'll be right beside you," Longarm told the town marshal.

Anne Carter and Terry Bullea's saloon, the Golden Pick, was not as large as Longarm had expected, but it was handsomely furnished in scarlet and gold, almost like a whorehouse.

The tables were busy offering roulette, faro, a wheel of fortune, and seven tables of either draw or stud poker. Each of the poker tables, Longarm noticed, had a house dealer who did nothing but shuffle the cards and deal them out.

Noogie saw Longarm looking at the poker tables. He nudged his friend with an elbow and said, "The way those operate, the players each ante up a quarter. That money belongs to the house, but it's the house's only interest in the game. Annie don't take a cut from the winnings like most places do. And I can tell you, these games are stone-cold honest. There's no bottom dealing or anything like that. The house has no interest in who wins or how much. They take that ante and nothing else."

"Different," Longarm mused, reaching for a cheroot. Almost before he could get the twist bitten off and the cigar properly seated between his teeth there was a girl there offering a lighted match.

He puffed his cheroot alight and nodded his thanks to the girl, who was wearing a short skirt and a tight top, both red trimmed in gold.

The girls—there were at least eight of them working the floor—were all dressed in that uniform. They were attractive but nothing like the beauties at Terry Bullea's whorehouse.

"That one over there," Noogie said, pointing, "her name is Edith. She gives great head but she's a so-so fuck. If you want a wild ride, take Lily. She's the one standing near the piano there. She doesn't have the face but there's nothing wrong with her body. And Lordy, can she ever use it. She'll practically twist a man's dick off, she works those hips so fast. Lily is really something, I tell you. You'll be giving yourself a treat if you try her."

"I thought we came here to gamble," Longarm said.

Noogie grinned at him and winked. "Yeah, we can do some of that, too, if you like."

"Good, 'cause I'm heading for that table over there," Longarm told him.

"Listen, if you're not going to take Lily . . ."

Longarm clapped him on the shoulder and said, "No, not tonight. You go ahead. Have fun."

Noogie practically raised a dust he took off so fast headed toward Lily. Longarm, for his part, ambled over to a poker table where there was room for a fifth player across the table from a redheaded female dealer.

Longarm liked the arrangement at the Golden Pick. The house got its piece of the play but had no incentive to cheat since the dealer was not a participant and none of the players belonged to the house.

Longarm reached into his britches for some pocket change and contributed his ante.

The dealer nodded a welcome, shuffled, and offered Longarm the deck to cut before she began to very expertly distribute the pasteboards to each of the players in turn.

The same girl who had lighted his cheroot appeared at his side again. "Would you like a glass of rye, Marshal?"

"I would, thank you." It occurred to him that it was just a damned good thing he was not trying to hide his identity. It seemed like everyone in Deadwood already knew who he was, even knew what he liked to drink.

His drink arrived almost immediately. The rye was the same superior product that he had been served at Theresa's place. Longarm sat back, took a second taste, and picked up his cards.

Now this, Longarm thought, was a pleasant way to pass an evening.

Chapter 44

The following morning Noogie DiNunzio came into the café where Longarm was finishing his breakfast. He slid onto the stool beside Longarm's and waved to the cook, miming taking a drink of coffee, then turned to Longarm and said, "How'd you do last night?"

"Tolerable," Longarm told him. "I only lost two dollars and a half, but the liquor was good and the company pleasant enough. Where'd you disappear to for the whole evening?"

Noogie grinned at him. "You know damn good and well where I went."

"Lily?"

"Uh-huh." He shook his head, smiling. "I tell you, that girl is a wild one for sure."

"I guess we both of us had our fun then," Longarm said.

"I got a borrowed phaeton out front," Noogie said. "Clo and John Halley will meet you in front of the Fremont office. I told them seven o'clock sharp." He checked his watch. "It's not quite six thirty now so you have plenty of time to finish your breakfast."

"Me? As in singular? As in just the one o' us?" Longarm asked. "What are you gonna be doing? I thought you said you wanted t' go along."

"I do want to, but it turns out that I can't. Last night Annie told me they'll be taking a box of cash money over to the bank to deposit. She has her own guards, of course, but I always go with them. It's part of my job, Longarm. I hope you understand."

"I understand a man's duty, Noogie. These robberies took place outside your jurisdiction anyway, and a man has t' tend to business. I'll pick up Clovis an' Halley and we'll go see if we can learn anything. There's no real need for you t' be there."

"Thanks, hoss." Noogie stood, leaving his coffee untasted, touched the brim of his hat in salute and left.

Longarm went back to his pork chop and eggs.

"Right up there," Clo Sensabaugh said, pointing to a sandy wash about thirty yards ahead of the phaeton.

"Say, that's the same place I was robbed," John Halley put in. "I remember I just drove down into that wash. Next thing I knew they stepped out from that brush on the right."

"Same thing when I was robbed," Sensabaugh said. "I never saw 'em coming. Then they was right in front of my team, pointing those bloody awful double barrels right at my face."

"Exactly," Halley said.

Longarm brought the pair of handsome sorrels to a halt and set the brake.

"I tossed the strongbox down on that side there, and the one in front of me stepped aside and waved me on.

Later the strongbox was found. It had been broke open and the contents taken."

"Where was it found?" Longarm asked. "Was it there in the road where you dropped it?"

Halley shook his head. "Not mine."

"Mine, neither," Sensabaugh said. "It was dragged into the brush and left there."

"Were there horse tracks that you could tell had anything to do with the robbers?" Longarm asked.

Both men shook their heads. "Two things," John Halley said. "Firstly is the loose sand in the wash there. It doesn't take prints that you can tell anything from, just depressions in the sand if there is anything at all. The other is that this is the only road through Lead and into Deadwood. There's horse and mule and ox outfits coming through here all the time leaving all manner of prints wherever there's ground that will take them. You wouldn't be able to get a thing in the way of hoofprints here."

"That's true," Sensabaugh put in. "I know. I looked around myself the next time I was through. Couldn't see a damn thing."

Longarm grunted and pulled the phaeton off the road. He stepped down and walked the ground. He did not know what he was looking for exactly. He just knew that he wanted to look, wanted to try to get some idea of what these robbers were like and how they operated.

They had chosen a good spot for the robberies. The coaches would have been slowed by the deep sand in the wash. There was thick brush on one side of the road. On the other side, a hundred yards or so distant, there was a sheer bluff. Just on the other side of the wash the road curved around a stand of very old cottonwoods that blocked the line of sight from that direction. A coach coming in from the west would not be able to see what was ahead.

Longarm turned to the stagecoach drivers and asked, "Do you know if any outbound coaches have been robbed or any gold shipments?"

Both men shook their heads. "There would be no sense in robbing an outbound," Sensabaugh said.

"They ship ore," Halley explained, "not processed gold. That ore hasn't been refined yet so it would take a heap of the stuff to be worth anything at all. Most of it around here assays . . . what, Clo . . . thirty dollars to the ton or thereabouts?"

"Something like that, I think," Sensabaugh added. "For sure it wouldn't be worth robbing."

"And passengers leaving the district might or might not have anything in their pockets."

"But those payrolls, now that is something else."

Longarm grunted. He pondered for a moment. Then he nodded and returned to the phaeton.

He never heard the gunshot until after the bullet sizzled past practically beneath his nose.

Chapter 45

Longarm threw himself backward off the driving seat of the phaeton and into the passenger box. By the time he bounced off the front seat and onto the floor he had his Colt in hand.

Not that he expected the short gun to be of much use. The lapse of time between when he heard the bullet's passage and when he finally heard the report of the rifle—it almost had to be a rifle, he realized—was proof enough that the shooter was some distance away.

Worse, he could not tell which direction the shot came from. The sound of the gunshot could have reached him from the top of the bluff to his left. Or just as easily the rifle could have been fired from the more open country to his right and the sound bounced off the bluff. Either way it sounded like it was fired from his left, and there was no way he could know for certain.

Yet.

He peered over the side of the phaeton just as the rifleman fired again. This time he saw the faint puff of white smoke that even so-called smokeless powder gives off. It came from the top of the bluff. The shooter was not at the very closest point to the road, instead was firing from close to two hundred yards away.

This time instead of hearing the bullet pass close to him he heard the moist, meaty thump of a bullet striking flesh and one of the sorrels screamed as it went down in the traces.

The son of a bitch was nailing the phaeton in place.

Long enough to make a leisurely getaway? Probably, Longarm guessed.

Perhaps the son of a bitch thought he had killed Longarm. Perhaps he thought Longarm's dive for concealment was reaction to a mortal wound.

Furious, Longarm cocked his double-action .45, took very careful aim at the spot where he saw the puff of smoke making allowance for the distance and squeezed off five shots, reloaded, and fired another six.

He doubted his bullets came anywhere near the shooter. But he felt better about being able to shoot back anyway.

Finally he sat up and looked around. There was no sign of either Sensabaugh or Halley. And the near sorrel was down, the other animal stamping its feet and rolling its eyes in distress, probably at the smell of blood from its sorely wounded companion.

Longarm reloaded with the last of the cartridges he carried in his pockets, then risked standing in the phaeton. When no one shot at him again he stepped down to the ground and went to see to the wounded animal. It had been shot through the lungs and was dying in agony, its feet churning helplessly. Longarm put the beast out of its pain with another round from his .45, then he looked around and called, "Where are you boys? Come on in. We have work t' do."

He knelt and began the difficult process of pulling the harness off a dead horse.

Chapter 46

"Rig something up t' pull this dead horse off the road, will you please," he said to the two obviously unhappy stagecoach drivers. It had taken him several minutes to find them. Both men had been hiding well off the road and were not especially inclined to come out of their concealment even after he did locate them.

They stayed where they were until Longarm assured them that the hidden rifleman was gone. Not that he really knew, but it was a pretty good guess.

"What are you going to be doing while we do all the work?" John Halley asked.

Longarm glared at the man for a moment before he said, "First off, I'm the one as did all the work of getting that harness free. Secondly, I need t' hike up on top o' that bluff and see what I can see."

"You can't climb that face," Sensabaugh put in.

"No," Longarm told him, "but about a half mile down the hill ain't so steep. I can get up there, I think."

"That's a long way to walk," Halley said.

"An' you ain't the one as has t' walk it," Longarm told

him. "I am. An' it's gotta be done, so you two take care o' this horse while I go take a look up there."

"I don't like this," Halley said. "I think we should head back to Deadwood right away."

"Well shit, man, I don't like it, neither, but we'll all do what we got t' do. I won't be too awful long." He grinned. "Assuming we don't all of us get shot dead by whoever was up there. An' still could be."

He rather liked the way Halley's face went pale at the thought that the shooter could still be lying in wait up there.

Longarm fortified himself with a cheroot burning between his teeth, then started hiking. He had a long way to go.

Longarm grunted softly to himself. He had found the spot where the rifleman lay hidden. It was close to the rim of the bluff and avoided the prickly bed of juniper needles that would otherwise have seemed an even better location.

A pair of empty .44-40 cartridge cases gleamed in the midday sunlight. He cussed a little at that. The .44-40 was probably the most common chambering there was in all the popular rifles, Winchester, Kennedy, Marlin, and any other.

Out of habit he bent and picked them up. Just to make sure these were the shooter's brass and not something left behind by a gent out in search of some venison for supper, he sniffed them. The sharp, acrid scent of burned gunpowder was strong in Longarm's nostrils. The cartridges had been fired very recently. He slipped the empties into the coat pocket where his spare .45s had been.

He had not really expected to find anything of interest up here. And he had not. But he had had to look. Had to try.

Longarm turned and began the long walk back to where the very unhappy stagecoach jehus were waiting.

Come to think of it, he realized, the livery outfit was not going to like it much, either, what with losing a perfectly good horse in the deal. And the sorrels had been matched as to size and color, too. It would be a hard horse to replace.

He wondered if he could get one of the stagecoach lines to pay for the loss. If he had to put it on his expense report, some bean counter back east in Washington city would likely blow his top about it. Might get so agitated that he popped a sleeve garter, and wouldn't that be a tragedy.

Longarm smiled a little at the thought. He pushed his Stetson back on his head to allow a little air to reach his scalp and slowed his pace. There was no hurry now. Unfortunately.

Chapter 47

It was nearly dark by the time the lone sorrel dragged the phaeton back to town. Longarm stopped in front of the town marshal's office where a lamp was shining in the window to suggest that Noogie was there.

He turned in the seat and motioned Clovis Sensabaugh up onto the driving box, then handed the driving lines to the jehu.

"Turn this outfit in at the livery, will you? I just don't feel like facing them tonight."

Sensabaugh chuckled and said, "I don't blame you. Old man Gennovese can be hell on wheels when he gets his dander up."

"Tell him Fremont will pay for the dead horse, Clo." Longarm laughed and added, "An' I'll tell Bastrop that Fremont is paying an' Fremont that Bastrop is paying. That should make things interestin' for a while."

Longarm stepped down off the phaeton and waited while Sensabaugh drove away. Then he crossed the street and stepped inside the marshal's office.

Noogie was there, seated behind his desk with a cup of coffee and a stack of wanted fliers in front of him.

"Hello, Custis. I was just thinking about looking you up . . ."

"Look me up in the hotel? Or in them wanted posters?"

"Whichever fits," DiNunzio came back. "Nah, in the hotel, asshole. I think my turn to buy supper." With a wink he added, "Then we'll go over to Terry's place and see what we can see."

"You like that spot, don't you," Longarm said.

"Hell, yes. What man wouldn't. The girls are beautiful, and the price is right."

"I'm game," Longarm told him.

Over prairie dog stew and corn dodgers DiNunzio asked, "What did you find out this morning?"

Longarm frowned. "I didn't learn shit. But I did get shot at."

"Whoa! Shot? Tell me."

Longarm told him, then shook his head. "What I can't understand is why. I'm damn sure no threat to anybody up here. I haven't really learned anything, don't really know anything. So why would anybody bother taking a shot at me?"

"Could be unconnected with these robberies," Noogie offered. "Could be somebody wanted for something else entirely. Could be somebody in that pile of posters I got back at the office."

"Could be," Longarm grudgingly agreed. "But I doubt it." He sighed. "Oh, well. We'll figure it out. Or not."

Noogie dropped a coin onto the café table and shoved his chair back. "Are you ready? My balls are about to bust from thinking about Terry's girls."

"Lead the way. I'll be right behind you."

The whorehouse was a little busier this evening. Two

gents were seated on the plush upholstery being fed free drinks. Probably, Longarm guessed, a policy designed to loosen the purse strings when they chose to go upstairs.

Noogie very quickly had a perky little Mexican girl on one arm and a tall blonde on the other. The man did not seem at all intimidated by being outnumbered.

Longarm did not have time to sit before he was approached by the same lovely redhead who had greeted him two nights earlier. "Good evening, Agnes," he said.

The girl smiled. "You remembered my name."

"How could I forget?" He kissed her hand and allowed the girl to lead him to a chair that was set a little apart from the others.

"Rye whiskey, yes?" she asked.

"Rye whiskey, yes," he agreed.

Agnes flowed away—he swore the girls walked in such a way that it somehow did not seem that they were walking, more like they glided across the floor—to the sideboard. She returned moments later with a tumbler of rye and a plate of smoked oysters.

"Miss Theresa will be so very sorry to have missed seeing you again," Agnes said.

"She's away?"

Agnes nodded. "She and Dennis are at the casino this evening. With Miss Theresa's friend Anne."

"Ah. At the Golden Pick," he said. "I'd forgotten. Are Miss Carter and Miss Bullea partners? Or just friends?"

"I don't really know about their business arrangements," Agnes said. He thought the girl was lying—and was not very good at it—but he could not see why she would bother. Surely there was no reason why he would care. "I do know they are very good friends." She lowered her voice and whispered, "*Very* good friends. If you know what I mean."

"You mean . . . ?"

Agnes nodded. "Yes. But don't tell anyone that I said so, I beg you. We aren't supposed to know about that."

"It don't matter," Longarm said. "There's no reason I should care."

Nor did he. It did not matter at all to him who, or what, Theresa Bullea liked to fuck. He knew she was awfully good at it. And that she especially liked to have her pussy licked. Perhaps Anne Carter had something to do with that.

And Dennis was with them? That conjured up all manner of interesting combinations.

"Tell me, Marshal," Agnes said, drawing his attention back to her. "Would you like to see our upstairs rooms? I seem to recall you didn't go upstairs when you were here before." She smiled and took his arm.

Why not, he told himself. "Sure, honey. You just lead the way."

He looked around, but Noogie and his pair of girls had already disappeared.

Longarm glanced down at his redhead and decided that he could make do with just one girl tonight.

Chapter 48

Come morning Longarm's mouth felt like someone snuck in during the night and stuffed it with cotton. With dirty cotton, at that.

He was almost pissed off that Agnes looked as fresh as when he arrived the evening before. He gave the girl a hug and a kiss on the forehead, having forgiven her for looking so cheerful at such an hour.

"What time'zit?" he mumbled, looking at the daylight coming through the bedroom window.

"Does it matter?" Agnes asked.

Longarm thought about that for a moment but had to conclude that it really did not matter at all. "No," he said, "reckon not."

"Come downstairs," Agnes said, lifting her gown and pulling it over her head. A quick tie of her sash as she was fully dressed, or at least as much so as she needed to be. "We have breakfast, you know."

"I didn't know."

"Oh, yes. For special gentlemen only."

"An' I'm a special gentleman?"

Her smile was kittenish. "I certainly think so. Come now. Get dressed and we shall go down to see the others."

"Nice touch," he said.

"Miss Theresa says we should always treat our gentlemen as if they were our own dear fathers or brothers," the pretty girl said.

"I hope you didn't . . . uh, never mind that thought." He pulled on his clothes, stamped into his boots, and collected his Stetson. "I'm ready," he said.

"Then come. We will join the others."

The smell of bacon and sausage greeted them in the stairwell. It was good enough to get his stomach to rumbling, and he was sorry now that he had not stayed over the last time he was here. Although come to think of it, he had not been invited that time. Apparently he was now officially a "special gentleman."

They went back to the big dining room where Noogie, Tom Bligh, and one other man were seated in comfort, surrounded by Theresa's girls and obviously enjoying more than the hotcakes, eggs, and breakfast meats that were being offered on silver salvers.

Theresa Bullea was seated at the head of the table. She wore a frilly gown and looked every inch the lady of the manor. "Good morning, Marshal," she said with a smile. "I am so very sorry that I was not here to greet you last night. Did my dear Agnes make you comfortable?"

"Very," he said, taking the chair that was offered. Agnes held it for him although he somehow thought that was supposed to be the other way around.

The redhead quickly served him, piling his plate first

with hotcakes and eggs, then offering bacon, sausage patties, and slabs of ham.

"What, no fried taters?" he joked.

"Oh, I am sorry. I shall have Cook make you some at once." She started to turn away but Longarm grabbed her by the wrist. "I was jokin', honey. Set down an' have your breakfast."

"If you are sure . . ."

"I'm sure," he said.

"Longarm," Noogie said. "Now aren't you glad you came to Deadwood?"

"Noogie, I'll get glad when I have those stagecoach robbers behind bars where they belong."

"Do you have a good prospect of that, Marshal?" Bligh asked around a mouthful of biscuit and red-eye gravy.

"Well, sir, I can't really say about that," Longarm told the banker.

"Oh, really, Marshal, we are among friends here. Just us and the ladies."

"As you say, sir. But the truth is that I don't know anything more now than I did when I first got here. I wish I could tell you somethin' positive, but I just don't have anything positive t' tell." Longarm reached for a biscuit and the bowl of sweet butter. Damn, but Theresa knew how to put on a feed.

"Where next, Custis?" Noogie asked.

Longarm shrugged. "Reckon I'll go interview everybody again." He looked at Bligh and said, "That includes you, Tom. I'll come by later this mornin' and talk t' you about it." He shook his head. "Damnit, there's a leak someplace. Has t' be. That's the only way those sons o' bitches could know what coaches to hit." To Theresa he said, "Thank you for this breakfast. Best one I can remember in ever so long."

"I am pleased that you enjoy it, Custis."

"Would somebody please pass that there platter o' ham?"

Chapter 49

On a whim Longarm walked over to the investment bank to speak with them there. When he entered the quiet building his reception was like he was trying to intrude on a very exclusive gentleman's club. And unlike at Theresa Bullea's whorehouse, he most definitely was not regarded as a gentleman here.

The fellow who hurried to meet him just inside the door had the air of a man who was rushing to put out the trash. The cheeky son of a bitch even took Longarm by the elbow and tried to steer him back toward the door.

"Whoa up, old son," Longarm said with a patently phony smile as he set his weight to resist the tug on his arm. "I'm goin' in that way, not back where I just been."

"I don't believe you are a customer, and . . ."

"And I'm gonna swat you like a fly if you don't leave me be, damnit," Longarm snapped.

"But . . ."

"I'm a deputy United States marshal, mister, an' you do *not* want t' piss me off. Now take me to the boss o' this outfit an' do it pronto."

"Yes, sir, I . . . yes." The fellow—he could not have weighed much more than a hundred pounds soaking wet and could not have budged Longarm on his best day—let go of Longarm's elbow and led the way into the depths of the dark and eerily silent bank.

George Conway was bald and beefy and no help at all. "Yes, we accept deposits of cash, Marshal," he explained, "but those are rare."

"Payroll money?" Longarm asked.

"Not usually although sometimes one of our more, um, prosperous customers will have some coinage left over from their payroll accounts. And of course we do business with several establishments that deal in large amounts of small coin. There are not many of those, as you might imagine."

"Yes," Longarm said. "That's exactly what I would imagine."

Conway seemed to have no idea that Longarm's remark was sarcasm. Longarm wondered if the man took his tie off when he fucked his wife. If he fucked his wife. If he had a wife.

"You're aware of the stagecoach robberies?" Longarm asked.

"I am, sir."

"Do any of your, um, deposits correlate to those robberies, Mr. Conway?"

"They do not."

"Then I thank you for your time."

"Mr. Perkin will see you out," Conway said, bowing and backing away to go do whatever it was that people like that went and did.

Longarm went back out onto the street and turned toward the next closest bank. He was greeted by a shout and the sight of Noogie DiNunzio running down the street, revolver in hand.

"What's up, Noogie?" Longarm shouted, breaking into a run to catch up with his friend.

"It's Tom Bligh," Noogie shouted over his shoulder. "He's been shot."

Longarm stretched his legs and got to the bank's doors only half a step behind DiNunzio.

Chapter 50

Bligh lay on the stone flooring of his bank. He had been dead for some time as the coldness of his flesh testified. A pool of scarlet blood would likely lend a permanent stain to the floor.

The man had been shot twice, once in the heart and another in the face.

"Powder burns," Longarm said. "He was shot from close up."

"He was shot by somebody he knew and trusted," DiNunzio said.

"How d'you know that, Noogie?" Longarm asked, unmindful, at least for the moment, of the crowd that was gathering around the body.

"When he was on the job, Tom was a careful man. Suspicious, you might even say. Leroy there says Tom stayed behind when the bank closed its regular hours, and the body is cold. He's been dead almost that long, I'd say. That means he opened up after hours. And Tom wouldn't do a thing like that unless he was confident about the person he was letting in."

Longarm grunted. "Interesting," he said. "But why?"

Noogie shrugged. "He didn't have time to write on the floor in his blood or nothing like that. I wisht he'd've left a note or something."

"Yeah, that'd be convenient. Reckon we'll just have t' make do with . . ." He looked up at one of the bank employees hovering over the body. "Your name is Leroy?"

The bank clerk nodded vigorously, his Adam's apple bobbing. "Leroy White, Marshal."

"You found the body?"

"Yes, sir. When I came to work this morning. The door was unlocked, like always. Mr. Bligh always got to the bank before anyone else. He opened up and left the door open for the rest of us. So I didn't think anything suspicious until I got inside and saw Mr. Bligh lying there. I could see all that blood, and I've seen dead men before. I was in the war, so I saw lots of them."

"Was he expecting anyone when you closed up last night?"

The clerk shook his head. "Not that I know of, Marshal. But I tell you what I can maybe do. I can look through the ledgers and see if anything was deposited after hours or if there were any withdrawals. I have to figure out what, if anything, was stolen anyhow."

"You can do that?" Longarm asked.

"Marshal, we don't get so very many deposits to begin with, and I handle all the routine transactions at the window. If Mr. Bligh took in anything significant, I would see it. And of course I'll want to look and see what might have been stolen by Mr. Bligh's killer."

"Good idea, Mr. . . . you said your name is White?"

"Yes, sir. It might take me a little while, but I'll look into all those things and get back to you quick as I can."

"Thanks." Longarm stood, his knee joints cracking.

He reached for a cheroot and took his time about lighting it while DiNunzio and an undertaker talked about what was to be done with the body. Then Longarm and DiNunzio left the bank together.

"Any idea who will take charge of the body?" Longarm asked. "Did the man have family someplace?"

"Oh, Tom has family right here in Deadwood. He's . . . that is he *was* . . . married, you know."

"He was? But he was spending time at Theresa's place."

Noogie turned his head and spat into the street. "Tom only went over to Theresa's when there was something special going on. To relax his nerves. Things like an audit of his books . . . this is only a branch of a Cheyenne bank, you know."

"No, I didn't realize that."

"Oh, yes. Tom always was nervous when he was audited. Not that he was allowing any shenanigans. Not at all. He was just fussy about that sort of thing. Or any large transactions. He was nervous about those, too."

"Like large payroll amounts coming in?" Longarm asked.

"I suppose so," Noogie said. "I wouldn't know for sure. Tom never mentioned those. Not to me nor anyone else that I know of."

Longarm grunted and thought for a moment. Then he said, "I'd best get back to what I was doing. I'm reinterviewing everyone at the banks and the stage line offices. I want to talk with everyone Bligh had contact with. All that I can find anyway." He grunted, the sound as much growl as grunt. "I'm no closer to finding those robbers now than I was when Billy Vail sent me up here."

"I'd go with you, Custis, except I have to notify Mary about Tom being killed and open an investigation report on the murder."

"All right," Longarm said. "Lunch later?"

"Sure. Come by the office when you're ready." Noogie made a sour face. "I'll be stuck there for quite a while."

Longarm flicked his cigar butt into the street, wheeled to his left, and stepped down off the boardwalk. He had to wait for an ore dray to pass, then he crossed over and headed for the third bank in Deadwood.

This was not turning out to be a very productive day, he thought.

Chapter 51

Noogie DiNunzio dropped his fork beside his plate and patted his belly. "Where do you go now, Custis?"

"Over to Theresa's house," Longarm said. "You should come, too."

Noogie raised an eyebrow.

Longarm leaned back and reached for a cheroot. Once it was streaming smoke he said, "I ran into Leroy White on my way over here. He said Bligh did take in a deposit last night. From Theresa Bullea. Apparently she has her accounts there. Very large accounts that justify them keeping the bank open for her now and then. Her and her partner Anne Carter. They share their bank accounts."

"That seems a strange arrangement."

"Maybe, but it's what they do. White said it wasn't unusual for Theresa or sometimes Anne to want to do their business after hours, when there wouldn't be any customers in the bank."

Noogie picked up his fork and used it to swirl around in the grease that was congealing on his plate. "I think we need to talk to Theresa. Ask her if she saw anyone lurking outside when she left or if anybody else came in while she was there."

"I also want t' talk to any girl Tom was partial to on his visits. Could be he let something slip. Pillow talk, I think that's called," Longarm said. "If he did, an' she said something to anybody else, that could be the way the robbers knew t' hit the inbound stage." He took a swallow of the coffee that was now growing cold in the bottom of his cup. "It wouldn't be hard for somebody t' figure out which stage line carried payrolls for what mines. If they could get a handle on it by way of watchin' to see when Tom Bligh visited Miss Theresa or . . . I dunno . . . could be some other tell to tip them off to shipments coming to the other bank."

"We can ask," Noogie said. "There might be something."

"Aye, it never hurts to ask." Longarm dug into his britches and came up with a gold two-dollar-fifty-cent coin. He waved to get the waiter's attention so he could get change for their two dinners.

"She won't be open this early," Noogie said.

"I ain't going there as a customer, y'know. I figure t' bang on the door until somebody comes t' open up."

"You don't mind if I go with you?"

"O' course not," Longarm said. "The murder is your case, after all. It's the robberies that I'm here about."

Noogie stood, pushing his chair back from the table. "Let's go, hoss."

Chapter 52

It took a considerable amount of pounding on the door to rouse someone inside the whorehouse. Finally a short blonde showed up, wrapped in a kimono and sleepy-eyed.

"What do you want at this hour?" she said.

"It's one o'clock in the afternoon, Gail," Noogie told her.

"Yeah. That's what I meant. It's too early."

"We need to see Theresa," Longarm put in, stepping uninvited through the front door and into the vestibule.

"I'm sorry, sir. Miss Theresa isn't here."

"Dennis then," Longarm said.

"Mr. Dennis isn't here, either, just now."

"Well, who the hell *is* here?" Longarm snarled.

"There's just us girls," the little blonde said.

Longarm turned to DiNunzio and said, "Did Tom have a favorite?"

"I never gave much thought to it, but I suppose he did. There were times when he used other girls though."

"Any one in particular when there was a shipment of cash coming in?" Longarm asked.

"I think . . . I think that Chinese girl, maybe. I remember Tom saying once that she didn't have much English. Just a phrase or two and them having to do with whoring and the men's wants." DiNunzio turned to the blonde and said, "Lotus. Where would she be?"

"In bed, where any sensible person should be at this hour," the girl said.

"Get her," Noogie said.

"Better yet," Longarm put in, "take us to her." He looked at Noogie and in a low voice said, "We wouldn't want her t' slip off and be all of a sudden hard t' find."

"Right," Noogie said. He looked at the girl. "Well?"

"Miss Theresa might not like this."

"That don't matter. We're gonna see Lotus right now one way or another. It would be better if we was to do it without busting anybody's heads."

The blond girl frowned. But she motioned them toward the staircase. "Lotus has the last room on the right."

Longarm took the steps two at a time while Noogie followed behind. He waited for DiNunzio to catch up, then twisted the doorknob without knocking. The door was unlocked. It opened to a room that was decorated in red and black.

The bed was rumpled and at first Longarm thought Lotus had somehow gotten wind of the visit and got away ahead of them. Then he saw a tangle of black hair resting on the pillow, almost drowned in a sea of satin.

The girl was tiny. She was almost swallowed up by the very ordinary-sized bed.

Longarm strode to the side of the bed and pulled the satin covers back.

Lotus, it seemed, preferred to sleep in the nude. In repose she looked like a porcelain doll, small and exquisite with gleaming black hair and pale flesh. She had tits like the saucers that come with little girls' tea party sets. The lips of her pussy showed red inside a nest of black hair.

Longarm got a hard-on looking at her, and he could not help but notice that Noogie did, too. DiNunzio's pants stood out in front of him.

Longarm bent down and shook the girl by the shoulder. "Wake up, Lotus. We got t' talk with you."

"Go away, you bastard. Can't you see I'm trying to sleep here?"

Longarm blinked. This was a girl who had practically no English?

"Well, I'll be a son of a bitch," Noogie said. "She speaks English as good as you or me. I remember Tom telling me once what a pleasure it was being with this girl because he could tell her anything and not have to worry about her understanding anything he said."

"Anything like, um, the schedule for payroll shipments to his bank?" Longarm said.

"That damn sure could be," Noogie said. He leaned down and told the girl, "Get up and get dressed, you. Me and my friend the U.S. marshal and you are all three going over to the town marshal's office where we expect to get some information from you, Lotus."

"I don't want to go," the girl said. In perfect English.

"Honey, I didn't ask do you *want* to go," Noogie said. "I said that we're going. Now do you want to walk over like a normal person or do you want to go in handcuffs like somebody who is fixing to do some jail time?"

"Give me a minute then, damnit. I got to get dressed and brush my teeth first. Then maybe I can go with you."

Longarm stepped back away from the side of the bed.

There was a straight chair by the bedside table. He swept Lotus's kimono off of it and sat down. Noogie perched on the foot of the girl's bed.

"We'll wait," both said, almost at the same time.

Chapter 53

The girl came with them voluntarily if more than a little unhappily. They walked together over to the town marshal's office, where Noogie sat the girl onto a straight chair in front of his desk.

Longarm leaned against a file cabinet and let Noogie take the lead in his own office.

The town marshal took out a pair of handcuffs and fastened the girl's left wrist to the rear leg of the chair she was sitting on. Then he went around to the front of his desk and bent down to open a bottom drawer. He brought out a pint bottle of whiskey and a flat leather cosh that was weighted with lead shot at the business end.

DiNunzio pulled a pair of calfskin gloves from another drawer and drew them on. Finally he uncorked the whiskey, which at first confused Longarm since Noogie did not drink hard spirits. Instead of taking a pull at the bottle himself he offered it to Lotus.

When she shook her head he said, "You might want to take a drink or two. This will hurt less maybe."

The girl's eyes went wide when Noogie picked up the

cosh and stepped around the desk to stand beside and slightly behind her.

"Wait," Longarm said. "Before you start in on her, let me have a little talk with her. Nice an' friendly like."

Noogie grunted, but he said, "You can try if you like, but my method is more likely to get something out of her."

"Give me the chance. If she doesn't open up for me, you can do it your way."

By that time the Chinese girl looked like she was about to break down in tears. She was trembling and her breath was rapid and shallow.

Longarm dragged another straight chair over from the side of the room and set it close to the chair where the girl was secured. He had a sudden thought, considering how good her English had gotten when she was half asleep. "What's your real name, honey?" he asked.

She hesitated for only a moment before she said, "My name is Frances Suh."

"Thank you, Frances. Now the thing is, me and Marshal DiNunzio here think you might know some things we're interested in. It's only fair for me to tell you that you might be in trouble with the law here. Dependin' on what we learn here t'day there's three things might could happen to you.

"One is that we could find you t' be implicated in the murder of Mr. Thomas Bligh, a gentleman I believe you know pretty well."

"Murder?" The word came out as a squeak.

"If you're convicted of murder . . . an' you should know that anybody who's no more'n an accessory to murder is subject to the same penalty under the law as somebody that pulls the trigger . . . if that happens, Frances, you're either hang or spend the rest o' your life behind bars."

"Behind . . . God, no."

"The second thing that could happen, Frances, is that you could be charged with bein' an accessory to theft of U.S. gov'ment mail. For that you'd get maybe five t' fifteen years in prison."

Frances Suh was crying now. "Could I have a drink of that whiskey. Please?"

Longarm nodded, and Noogie handed the bottle to her. She raised it to her lips and took a man-sized pull at it.

"Or, lookin' on the bright side," Longarm said, "you could be named a cooperating witness an' get off complete."

"Really?" she sobbed.

Longarm nodded. "Really."

"What . . . what do you want to know?"

Longarm smiled and sat down beside her.

Chapter 54

"Don't you need a court order or somethin'?" Longarm asked as they walked.

"This is kind of a small town, hoss. They trust me here. If we decide we need a search warrant, the magistrate will give me one. If we don't find anything, well, no harm done."

"If you're satisfied with it, Noogie, so am I."

Once again Longarm pounded on the whorehouse door until the same little blonde came to open it, looking just as sleepy and annoyed as she had the first time they called.

"Has Miss Theresa or Dennis come back yet?" Noogie asked.

"No, they . . . hey! Where do you think you're going?"

Longarm and DiNunzio barged past the girl and headed down the hallway that led to Theresa Bullea's private quarters. The door was locked, but a pocketknife served to jimmy it open.

"You can't do that," the girl yelped behind them.

"So call the police," Longarm told her. To Noogie he said, "The chifforobe. That's where t' look first."

It, too, was locked, but the same pocketknife served to open it.

"Aw, shit," DiNunzio moaned when they got the wardrobe open. "I didn't want to see those there, never mind what the girl said."

"Had t' be," Longarm said. "Frances said the onliest one she talked to about what Bligh told her was the boss an' Dennis. Had t' be them." He reached into the wardrobe and pulled out both an oversized linen duster and a flour sack with eyeholes cut in the fabric.

Standing in a back corner of the chifforobe were two sawed-off twelve-gauge scatterguns, wicked enough to make any man think about his maker if he was staring into those large tubes.

"Shit!" Noogie repeated. "I tell you what, though. If Terry and Dennis was into it, then so was Annie. What one of them does, they all of them do."

Longarm looked toward the doorway where the blonde was hanging just in the corridor leading to the front door. She bolted when he started toward her, but he broke into a run and grabbed the back of her kimono before she could get away.

"I'm thinkin', Noogie, that we'd best walk this young thing over to your jail an' put her in with the other'un for the time being."

"Right. Uh, do you think maybe Tom worked it out in his own mind and that's why he was killed? He would have opened the door for Terry or Annie either one."

"That's something we may never know, but I'd say it's

a mighty good guess. C'mon now. Let's put this one in where she can't go warn anybody. Then you and me will see can we find our robbers."

"And murderers," Noogie added.

"Ain't that the damn truth."

Chapter 55

They had barely stepped onto the front porch when the blond girl shouted, "Run, Miss Theresa, run!"

Longarm looked in the direction the girl was looking. Theresa Bullea and Dennis were just emerging from an alley half a block down. If the girl had not shouted, Longarm doubted they ever would have spotted the pair.

"Hold her," he snapped at Noogie and set off at a run toward Terry and Dennis.

Theresa bolted back into the alley, but Dennis decided to fight it out then and there. He palmed a revolver and snapped a shot that whined over Longarm's head.

Was Dennis the shooter who tried to plug him when he drove the two jehus out to the scene of the robberies? There was a damn good chance of it.

While that thought was flashing through his mind, Longarm's Colt was in his hand, almost without conscious thought. He saw the threat and he reacted.

"Stop, Dennis. I don't wanta kill you." And that was the truth. He wanted information from the man, not blood.

Dennis did not give him a choice. The whorehouse bouncer fired a second time.

The man should have stuck to beating up on drunks, Longarm thought as he took quick aim and returned the gunfire.

Dennis went pale as a .45 slug ripped into his belly. His revolver's muzzle sagged toward the ground and discharged harmlessly beside his boot.

Longarm made sure with a more carefully aimed shot that took Dennis in the forehead, snapping his head backward and putting the man down in the dirt.

Longarm broke into a run then. Theresa had several long seconds to try to escape.

He did not want her to succeed. The bitch had played him for a fool, knowing why he was in Deadwood but taking him into her bed.

He pounded into the alley mouth, jumping over the dying bouncer, faithful to the end.

Theresa surprised him again. Instead of trying to get away she was waiting for him not ten feet distant in the shadows of the alley.

A blossom of fire erupted and a bullet sizzled past close to his head.

Longarm did not take the time to think about what he should do. He reacted automatically, the Colt that was still in his fist returning her fire.

Theresa crumpled to the ground amid the litter of trash in the alley.

He rushed forward. Before he did anything else he kicked the derringer out of her hand. Then he knelt.

"I thought . . . I thought . . ."

Longarm never learned what it was that Theresa thought. She died before she could complete the sentence, the light of life fading quickly from her wide, staring eyes.

Longarm heard footsteps behind him. He wheeled to face them, but it was only Noogie.

"Both of them are gone?" DiNunzio asked.

Longarm nodded. "Not the way I would've wanted it but . . . yeah."

"Then before word of this travels to the next block I think we'd best go arrest Annie Carter," Noogie said. "At the very least she's in for conspiracy. I'm not sure we can make anything else stick. You want this for federal filing?"

"You can have it if you like, Noogie. I don't think I'd enjoy escorting her back to Denver for trial anyway."

Noogie grinned. "Hell, hoss, I'll take her. It'll look good for me to have cleared up Tom's murder so quick."

"Then before we set in to countin' those chickens we'd best go put the cuffs on Annie. An' set Frances loose, I think. After all, she did what we wanted. Wouldn't hardly be fair to put her in the jug now."

"I tell you what then, hoss, you can do me the favor of escorting Frances Suh out of my jurisdiction for me. And, uh, you might want to know that according to Tom that little Chinee girl is a mighty good fuck."

"You have a dirty mind, Noogie."

"Positively filthy," DiNunzio agreed.

But Longarm could not help but savor a memory that flashed into his mind, that being a picture of Frances Suh lying naked and lovely on those satin sheets.

He smiled. It was a long way down to Cheyenne where the girl could catch a train. There was no telling what might happen between here and there.

Watch for

**LONGARM AND THE
CRY OF THE WOLF**

the 412th novel in the exciting LONGARM
series from Jove

Coming in March!

And don't miss

**LONGARM AND THE
AMBUSH AT HOLY DEFIANCE**

Longarm Giant Edition 2013

Available from Jove in February!

LONGARM

GIANT-SIZED ADVENTURE FROM AVENGING ANGEL LONGARM.

BY TABOR EVANS

penguin.com/actionwesterns

M456AS0812

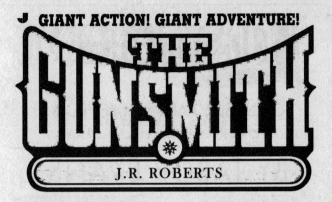

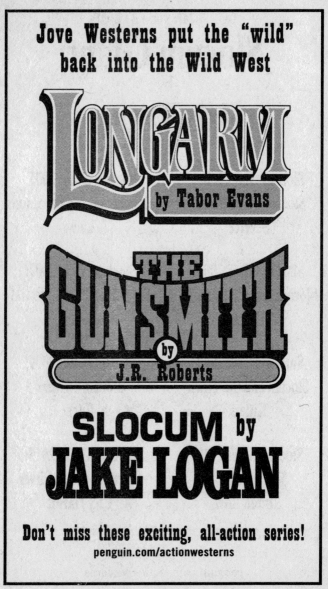